Miss Merry's Christmas

CALLIE HUTTON

Miss Merry's Christmas

COPYRIGHT © 2012 by Callie Hutton

Re-release November 2013

Cover design by Book Graphics

This book is a work of fiction. The names, characters, places and incidents are the product of the author's imagination and are used fictitiously. Any resemblance to actual events, business establishments, locales or persons, living or dead, is entirely coincidental.

All rights reserved. No part of this publication may be reproduced, stored in a retrieval system, or transmitted by any form, or in any means (electronic, mechanical, photocopying, recording, or otherwise) without the prior written permission of both the copyright owner and the publisher. The only exception is brief quotations in printed reviews.

The scanning, uploading or distribution of this book via the internet, or via any other means without the permission of the copyright owner and publisher is illegal and punishable by law. Please purchase only authorized electronic editions, and do not participate in or encourage electronic piracy of copyrighted materials. Your support of the author's rights is appreciated.

For more information, visit the author's website: www.calliehutton.com

ISBN:1480133647
ISBN-13:9781480133648

ABOUT THE BOOK

David Worthington, Duke of Penrose dislikes Miss Meredith Chambers, the American governess who accompanied his new wards. He especially detests his attraction to the insufferable woman, and is anxious for her replacement to arrive. Merry is thrilled when the Dowager Duchess Penrose hires her as a companion. Now she can stay with her beloved charges. But can she ignore how her heart thumps when the pompous duke gets close? Two people determined to ignore each other, despite the pull between them, and the sparks that fly whenever they're together.

DEDICATION

To Aunt Mary. Even after all these years, I still miss you.

ACKNOWLEDGMENTS

No man is an island, and no book is written by just the author. Critique partners, beta readers, and editors all play a part in the final product.

My critique partner, Romance Author, Char Chaffin, slapped my hand every time I overused a word or phrase. She brutally cut me off, with no remorse. I love her.

My beta readers, Warren Greene, Romance Author Ella Quinn, and Romance Author Ally Broadfield offered innumerable suggestions and advice. They even caught a mistake or two.

And a special thanks to Ella, who pulled my arse from the flames more than once when I blundered in relating details of Regency life. Any mistakes are mine, and mine alone.

CHAPTER ONE

Hamptonshire, England
October, 1813

Miss Meredith Chambers took a deep breath and smiled at the two little girls staring up at her with wide eyes. "Well, it appears we're here."

Her smiled faltered when they both grabbed her legs and hid their faces in her skirts. "What's this?"

"I don't want to live here," Charlotte, the older of the sisters, wailed.

"Me neither," Clare echoed.

Merry dropped to her knees and pulled them both close. "You are the duke's wards. He is a very important man, your father's best friend. You will love living here."

Two curly, blond-haired heads shook furiously.

"Madam?" The front door of the massive house opened, and a tall, thin butler, his nose as long as the rest of him, glared down at them. "His Grace awaits you in the library."

Merry stood and patted her hair, which had come loose from her knot. Well, no time to fuss with it now. She took one step forward, dragging the two girls with her.

The sound of the well-sprung coach that delivered them, its wheels clattering on the cobblestones, rang in her ears, the last link to their old life.

"Girls, release my legs, I am unable to walk."

They clung harder, causing her to shuffle along like an invalid. When they reached the bottom of the steps, Merry wrapped an arm around each small girl, lifted them, and climbed the steps.

The butler viewed the group without expression. "This way if you please."

Winded, Merry followed the man, still dragging her charges.

Goodness, the house was huge. The marble entrance hall was filled with delicate tables, over-stuffed Queen Anne chairs, and an immense clock, its sound almost as loud as her pounding heart.

"Madam? Do you wish assistance?"

Realizing she gaped like a ruffian from the street, she attempted to step forward, still impeded by the girls. "Ladies, you must let me go." They clung tighter. She flashed a smile at the butler, whose countenance remained impassive, leaving her to wonder if a smile ever graced his stoic face.

Despite her best intentions, Merry twisted back and forth, amazed as she took in her surroundings. Plush carpets, silk wall coverings, priceless lamps, all reminding her of the wealth and status of the girls' guardian. Her nose smacked into something solid as the butler came to an abrupt stop, but her body, with her two charges still attached firmly to her limbs, did not.

Lips twitching, but maintaining his austere demeanor, the butler opened a large wooden door with elaborate carvings, and sniffed before announcing, "Lady Charlotte Spencer, Lady Clare Spencer, and Miss Meredith Chambers."

The girls clung harder, making it practically impossible for Merry to enter the room. She dragged one limb, then the other, until she reached the massive oak desk. Breathless from her effort, she looked up into the most arresting brown eyes, with specks of gold, she'd ever seen. Above the eyes, sharp black eyebrows rose almost to the hairline of wavy black hair. Below the eyes an aristocratic nose led to sensual lips drawn into a tight line.

"Your Grace." She puffed and attempted a clumsy curtsy.

The only sound in the room was the soft click of the door as the butler exited. Merry waited patiently to be invited to sit. Instead, the brown eyes kept staring at her, then leisurely slid their way down her person, and obviously from the additional tightening of his full sensual lips, finding her wanting.

Eventually, a long-fingered hand flicked in the direction of one of the two leather chairs in front of his desk. "You may sit."

Merry sat abruptly, feeling like a dog panting in front of its master. The two girls ended up on their knees on the floor, still buried in her skirts.

"Is there something wrong with the young ladies?" The deep voice rolled over her, setting her heart to pounding.

Merry grasped the girls' arms and attempted to pull them to their feet. They held tighter. "No, Your Grace. They're merely a bit anxious."

"Indeed."

How was it possible to put so much disapproval into one word?

After a moment, he settled back in his chair, his fingers clutching a quill pen he tapped on the desk. "I trust you had a pleasant journey?"

With all the liquid in her mouth dried up, she merely nodded.

"I understand from my solicitors you've had sole charge of the girls since their parents passed away a month ago?"

"Yes, Your Grace." Good. She was finally able to pry her mouth open.

"And you find it so difficult to control your charges that they do not sit as proper ladies?"

Heat rose to Merry's face and anger washed through her. The arrogant arse! "They're confused and a bit distressed." She bent and whispered furiously to the girls. "Please get up, His Grace is not happy."

"No." Two voices piped up, muffled in her skirts.

She smiled slightly at the duke and shrugged. If possible his eyebrows rose further, disappearing underneath the wave that rested against his forehead.

"It appears to me, Miss Chambers, that Lady Charlotte and Lady Clare have arrived into my keeping just in time." He pushed his chair back and stood. "I arranged for a governess to train them in proper behavior. She will instruct the girls in the skills necessary for a lady of their station." He waved his hand. "Sewing, French, watercolors, and so forth."

Merry stared at him, her jaw slack. Well over six feet, David, Duke of Penrose, was a sight to behold. Every inch the lord of the manor, his coat fit him as if it had been painted on. His white-on-white waistcoat hugged his impressive body above well-fitting tan breeches tucked into shiny black Hessian boots. A snow white, intricately tied cravat stood in stark contrast to his lightly tanned skin.

Lord Penrose rounded the desk and rested one hip on the edge, peering down at her, his foot swinging back and forth. "I shall allow a bit of transition time for the young ladies. You may stay on for a week or two. Then I will see you receive a generous stipend to tide you over until you can secure another position."

Two blonde heads popped up from underneath Merry's skirts. "No!"

* * *

Penrose studied the two anxious faces in front of him. So these were the girls that might have been his, had

Eleanor chosen him instead of Bedford years ago. He stopped his thoughts from wandering in that direction. He'd gotten over the defection of the lovely Lady Eleanor, but found it ironic that it was he who would raise her daughters, see them presented to Society, and married. *Life takes interesting twists and turns.*

Miss Chambers presented a whole other issue. Although pretty in a common sort of way, with her huge blue eyes and less than tidy golden blond hair, her inability to handle the most minor directives to his wards did not bode well. In fact, it appeared he was about to face a mutiny before he'd even had the chance to speak to the young minxes.

"So you do possess faces. And voices."

"Girls, curtsy to His Grace."

Studying him with suspicion, they did a quick bob, then took the chairs on either side of Miss Chambers. The older girl studied her lap, and the younger one stuck her thumb in her mouth and twirled a lock of her hair.

Penrose's gaze shifted to Miss Chambers, who had the grace to blush.

"They're not usually this shy, Your Grace, but it has been a difficult month for them."

"Take your finger from your mouth." The order, coming out a bit stronger than he'd intended, had two sets of young eyes peering at him in terror.

"Young ladies do not suck on their thumbs, or twist their hair." He shifted his gaze to Lady Charlotte. "And girls a few years away from being presented to the Queen do not stare at their laps when addressed."

Both girls returned to their positions on the floor, their heads again buried in Miss Chambers' skirts.

Penrose sighed. "Miss Chambers."

The woman raised her chin, eyes flashing, and regarded him. "Yes, *Your Grace.*"

He chose to ignore the sarcasm in her voice. "I would be remiss in my duties as guardian to allow you to continue to supervise their activities. It is clear to me you have no control over them. They do not possess even a hint of good manners, and certainly not the demeanor required of their station." He held up his hand as she opened her mouth to speak.

"As I mentioned before, you will be permitted to remain here at Penrose Hall for a week or two until the girls are settled in. I will be more than generous, so you will be able to take time in securing a new position." He slid off the desk, and moved to return to his chair.

"Wait just a minute, *Your Grace.*"

Penrose came to an abrupt stop. No one in his life had ever addressed him with such derision. And to think it came from a governess. Horror gripped him as he swung around. "Are you American?"

Miss Chambers stood, both girls entangled in her skirts. "Yes. I am an American. And you, Your Grace, are an arrogant Englishman."

Blood rushed to his face, his heart thumping at the insolence. Then, without thought, he threw his head back and roared with laughter. This sprite of a woman—this *American*—had just insulted him as no other in his entire life. Used to bowing and scraping from his peers, and flirting and admiration from women, he felt as though someone had opened a window and let in fresh air. However, as amused as he was at her behavior, she would still have to go. His charges needed a good, English governess to bring them to right.

"Miss Chambers, I will overlook your outburst and attribute it to your lack of proper upbringing. Lady Charlotte and Lady Clare are in dire need of direction that you apparently have not provided. As grateful as I am that you took them under your wing when their parents died suddenly, I must insist on you leaving them into the care of the governess I have secured for them who will arrive on the morrow. Once your presence is no longer needed to secure the cooperation of my wards, you will be released."

He walked to the far right corner of the room and pulled the bell. Miss Chambers studied him as they waited for the servant he'd summoned. Within minutes, a young nursery maid entered the room and bobbed. "Your Grace?"

"See that Lady Charlotte and Lady Clare are settled. I believe Miss Chambers has been assigned the room adjoining theirs for the time being." His arms crossed, he looked at the woefully inadequate governess. "The young ladies will have dinner in the nursery. I will expect you to present yourself in the drawing room at precisely eight o'clock to join myself, my brother, Lord Brandon, and my mother, the Dowager Duchess of Penrose, for dinner."

With that command, he strode from the room.

* * *

Merry took a deep breath to keep from racing after the prig and giving him a piece of her mind. *Lack of proper upbringing*, indeed. Duke or no duke, Penrose was arrogant, condescending, and contemptuous. He'd frightened the girls and affected a most unpleasant welcome. She glanced at them still huddled on the floor.

"Come, let's get settled in the nursery, and see what fine books and toys are there."

Charlotte and Clare stood and took her hands. The trio followed the maid out the door and up the stairs. Wherever the contemptuous man had gotten off to, she didn't see him the entire trip. And a trip it was. Even though her former employers, Lord and Lady Bedford, had an impressive home, this dwelling put it to shame. It would take her weeks to learn all the hallways, wings and sections of the place. Except, she reminded herself, the *lord of the manor* would be tossing her out on her arse in a week or two.

She sighed. Charlotte and Clare had been her charges for five years, and leaving them in someone else's care troubled her. They'd been a mere seven and four when

Lord and Lady Belford hired her during their trip to America. Their nanny had succumbed to a fever, and Merry was only too happy to leave her home behind, where all the young men who had paid her addresses had married elsewhere.

As the daughter of a professor, she'd been educated beyond the expectations of most young ladies, and in fact, most men as well. Although the young bucks who attempted to court her were charming, they lacked the spark she desired in a lifetime mate.

She'd spent hours discussing books, plays and music with her father. Proud of her sharp mind, he'd taught her philosophy, economics, history, and languages. She'd picked up French and German quickly. A duck out of water in her circle of female friends, who only conversed about the latest gossip, gowns, and young men, the chance to travel to England shortly after her father passed away seemed her salvation. At one and twenty, it had been time for a new direction.

"Miss, this is the nursery. If you will follow me, I'll show you to your chamber next door." The young maid swung open the door to a brightly colored schoolroom. Small wooden tables and chairs took up the center of the room. A bookcase lined the walls, with puzzles, games and slates stacked on the shelves. On the far side of the room, a door led to what appeared to be a sleeping chamber.

The girls left her skirts for the first time since they'd alighted from the carriage earlier, hurrying to discover the wonders of the bookshelves.

"I'm going to get settled in my bedchamber, which is right alongside this one." Merry addressed the girls, amused to see they barely acknowledged her as they flipped through books and pulled out puzzles.

The governess's room was as large as the nursery. Blue and white striped silk covered the walls, broken up by windows on two of the four walls, bathing the area in bright sunlight. A large canopied bed with a flowered quilt and numerous pillows caught her eye as she viewed the room. Her shoes sank into plush carpet. The huge fireplace stood cold, causing her to run her hands up and down her arms against the chill.

"I'll light a fire for you right away, miss," the young maid assured her.

"Thank you. That will be nice."

Merry wandered about the room, examining the dressing table and chair, the empty wardrobe, and more bookcases filled with books. Penrose might be an overbearing brute, but the family certainly took very good care of their governesses. Well, no matter, she wouldn't be here long. Since the new governess was due to arrive tomorrow, this would probably be Merry's only night in this splendid room.

Her stomach clenched as she recalled the conversation with the duke. He obviously held little regard for Americans. Well, this American was not going to bow and scrape. Let her English counterparts do that. She sniffed. The aristocracy meant nothing to her. Her previous employers had allowed leniency in their daughters' upbringing, and having them now subjected to all the mores and strictures of Polite Society almost brought her to tears.

* * *

Merry sat on the floor of the nursery, legs crossed, Charlotte and Clare on either side of her, the three heads bent over the storybook Merry read. This was her favorite time of the day, when dinner was over, the girls washed and dressed for bed, and an engrossing story holding them hostage until time to sleep.

A maid had come to assist her to dress for dinner earlier, but she told the girl she would eat with her charges, and would not be joining the duke's family in the dining room.

"And the prince charming swept her into his strong arms, and twirled her around the dance floor. 'Will you marry me, my princess?' he asked. 'Yes,' she responded, much to his delight."

She paused for effect, then sighed. "After the royal wedding, they lived happily ever after." She gently closed the book. "The end."

"I like that story," Clare said before slipping her thumb into her mouth.

"Me, too," Charlotte added, dreamy-eyed. "One day I will meet a prince charming, who will twirl me around the ballroom."

Her younger sister nodded, enthralled with Charlotte's dream.

"I will wear the most beautiful gown, with matching—"

Merry jerked her head up as the door to the nursery flew open and slammed against the wall. Like the wrath of God, the Duke of Penrose stood in the doorway, fire in his eyes, his hands fisted at his sides.

"Miss Chambers, I *ordered* you to join my family for dinner."

CHAPTER TWO

Penrose couldn't believe his eyes. The termagant sat crossed-legged on the floor, her skirts halfway up her limbs, practically to her knees. The hair that had begun its descent earlier now fell in clumps around her shoulders. Miss Chambers hadn't changed from her travelling gown, and as one stockinged foot peeked out at him, she'd apparently removed her shoes. A total disgrace, and completely unacceptable as an influence on his wards.

"Now you've gone and frightened the girls again." She regarded him from her position on the floor, not making the effort to stand and re-arrange herself.

Penrose drew in a deep breath through his nostrils and attempted to soften his expression. It wouldn't do for the young girls to fear him, or he'd never be rid of Miss Chambers. "I apologize, ladies, I did not mean to startle you." His eyes shifted in the direction of the governess. "May I have a word with you, Miss Chambers? Outside." He turned on his heel and left the room.

He paced the corridor waiting for her to join him. Hands behind his back, he tried to calm himself. She was an American, the land of savages. It would bode him well to remember that in his dealings with the woman. Why his friend, and, of all people, Lady Eleanor, had seen fit to allow Miss Chambers anywhere near their daughters was a mystery.

Finally, she stepped from the doorway, her hair pinned up, and his quick glance at her feet showed she'd put on her shoes as well. At least the woman had a smidgen of dignity.

"Is there a problem, Your Grace?" She stiffened her shoulders and regarded him.

"The problem, madam, is I instructed you to join my family tonight for dinner. At exactly eight o'clock." He withdrew his pocket watch. "It is now sixteen minutes past eight. And my maid tells me you informed her you already took your dinner with the young ladies."

"Correct. They are trying to get used to their new environment. I felt it would be in their best interests for me to forego a formal dinner with your family tonight, and spend the time with the girls."

"Whether that was a good decision or not is irrelevant since I requested you join us."

"Ah, Your Grace. That is where the problem lies. You see, you did not *request* that I join your family. As you stated a few moments ago, you *ordered* me to join you."

His eyebrows rose. "What is the difference?"

Miss Chambers sighed. "Exactly."

"What the devil does that mean? You are speaking in riddles, madam." He bent close to peer directly into her eyes. "I will allow this one bit of defiance, as it might have been wiser for you to share their dinner tonight." He rose to his full height. "However, in the future, I will decide what will be done with the young ladies, and you, Miss Chambers, will abide by my wishes as long as you are under my roof."

By God, it actually looked as though she fought to keep from smiling. The woman had managed to rile him up more than anyone else in his life thus far. Not wishing to give her any more time to vex him further, he pivoted and strode down the corridor.

* * *

Merry returned to the nursery. Neither girl had moved an inch. Charlotte stared at her lap, and Clare sucked her thumb, her fingers busy twirling a lock of hair that had come loose from her braid.

"Does the duke dislike us?" Charlotte asked.

Merry smoothed back the young girl's hair. "No, of course not. The duke was your father's dear friend. Most likely he is not used to young ladies."

"He sure doesn't like you, Miss Merry." Clare mumbled around her thumb.

"It is not that he doesn't like me, exactly. He wants what's best for you, and we disagree on what that is."

"Will he really make you leave?" Charlotte studied her with wide eyes.

"All right, girls. I think we've had enough conversation about the duke. It's past your bedtime, and we're all tired from our trip today. Let's say our prayers and off to bed with you."

* * *

Dowager Duchess of Penrose, known as Kitty to her close friends and family, glanced up from her place on the settee in the drawing room as her son entered. Eyes flashing, his body held rigid, he extended his arm to her. She rose and laid her hand on his arm, then they walked toward the dining room.

"Are we not waiting for Miss Chambers?"

He glared in her direction. "She will not be joining us this evening."

Lord Brandon, her younger son, chortled. "Don't tell me Miss Chambers has defied your edict?" As they settled in their places, he reached for his glass of wine, drained it, and held it out toward a footman.

"She has already taken dinner with her charges. I'm afraid you will all need to wait until tomorrow to make her acquaintance."

"What? She didn't grovel at your feet and scurry down here to do your bidding?" Lord Brandon's eyes danced with mirth. "I am truly anxious to meet this woman."

"She's an American," Penrose said through tightened lips, as though that explained it all.

"How very interesting." Kitty took a piece of roasted salmon from the serving plate the footman held. "I wonder what possessed Lord Bedford to hire a foreigner?"

"When he and Eleanor visited the colonies a few years ago, their nanny caught a fever and died. I imagine they must have felt quite desperate to engage the likes of Miss Chambers."

"Is she that bad?"

"Remarkably unsuitable. She has no sense of propriety, no appreciation for the world the girls will enter in a few short years. She's opinionated, stubborn and impertinent." He took a deep breath and attacked his food.

"Well. She has certainly gotten under *your* skin." Kitty smiled at the pique she rarely saw in her always-in-control eldest son.

"Nonsense. The woman doesn't trouble me at all. In any event, she'll be leaving soon."

"Leaving? Has she another position already?" Lord Brandon pushed away his half eaten dinner and signaled for more wine.

Penrose glared at his brother's actions. "Not that it is necessary to keep you apprised of my decisions, but to quell any curiosity on your part, Miss Chambers has a week or two to see the girls settled into their new routine. At that point I will give her a stipend sufficient enough to tide her over until such time as she can secure a new situation."

"Dear, do you suppose the girls will feel secure enough in that short period of time? I believe you told me this governess has been with the family for some time now."

"Don't concern yourself, Mother. Now let us enjoy

our dinner with a more pleasant topic."

Kitty smiled behind her wine glass. Whatever or whoever this Miss Chambers was, she'd gotten more of a reaction from Penrose than anyone she'd ever seen. At four and thirty, her son, very much *the duke*, kept his feelings and emotions well hidden. Even as a child, he'd been like his father, pompous and haughty, always aware of his station. She'd been waiting for years to see a crack in that armor, and it seems a cheeky American governess was the one to do it.

Yes, she definitely would need to meet Miss Chambers, and as quickly as possible. She took another sip of her wine and listened to Lord Brandon and Penrose argue over her younger son's latest escapade.

* * *

The next morning Merry summoned a maid to help her dress. After assuring the girls were busy with their meal under the watchful eye of the nursery maid, she left with instructions on how to find the breakfast room. She could probably wander around a bit and get there, but with her luck she would run into the duke who would find another reason to chastise her. What a stiff-necked man. Lord Bedford had been warm and friendly, Lady Bedford the same. But this man—this aristocrat—embodied everything she disliked of the upper crust.

She and Lord and Lady Bedford had agreed the girls would enjoy a carefree childhood. In another couple of years Lady Charlotte would begin preparations for her coming out, but until then the girls enjoyed the activities all young children should be allowed to engage in.

Once she arrived outside the breakfast room, Merry took a deep breath to quell her thumping heartbeat, then slowly opened the door. The duke sat at the head of the table, with a plate filled with kippers, eggs, fruit, toast and bacon steaming in front of him. A folded newspaper was positioned at his elbow. Aside from him, the room was empty. Her stomach tightened.

He rose at her entrance. "Miss Chambers. I hope you had a comfortable night's sleep."

"Yes, Your Grace. The governess's room is quite comfortable, a lovely room. Quite pleasing and cheerful. Shall I be vacating it today? Is this not the day the new governess arrives?" Good heavens, she was babbling. One look from those penetrating eyes and all rational thought left her head.

Penrose held out a chair for her, and after she slid into it, he returned to his seat. "Why don't we enjoy our breakfast, and then we will discuss the plans for the day?"

An older woman swept into the room, nodded at the duke who stood as a footman pulled out a chair. She sat across from Merry. "You must be Miss Chambers."

The duke regarded her with raised eyebrows. "Mother, I haven't seen you at the breakfast table in quite a while."

The woman dismissed him with a flick of her fingers. "I rose early and decided to join the family." She turned her attention to Merry, ignoring Penrose's stare.

"Yes, ma'am, I'm Miss Chambers."

"I am Dowager Duchess of Penrose, and I am delighted to meet you." She cast a bright smile and glanced in the direction of the duke who regarded her through slitted eyes.

The dowager was pale where Penrose was dark, her features striking rather than pretty. The enthusiasm in her expression brought beauty to her face. A light fragrance had emanated from her as she'd moved from the door to her seat, settling in comfortably. After what Merry had witnessed of the duke thus far, it was hard to reconcile this woman as his mother.

Merry sighed in relief. At least the entire family wasn't as arrogant as the duke. "And it is my pleasure to make your acquaintance, Your Grace."

"Ho. It appears our little governess has deigned to join us this morning." A man, perhaps a few years younger than the duke, but bearing him a striking resemblance nevertheless, strode into the room. He stopped before Merry, bowed slightly before taking her hand, and raising it slowly to his mouth as he stared into her eyes, kissed it. "I am Lord Brandon Worthington, brother, and unworthy heir apparent, to Penrose. At your service." He winked at her and moved to the sideboard to fill his plate.

"Another surprise visit at the breakfast table," Penrose mumbled.

"My dear," the young man spoke as he took the chair next to Merry, "I am delighted you are with us. You must tell me all about America. Is it true the savages run amok, killing people at will?"

Her smile vanished. The misconceptions she'd run into during her years in England amazed her. She thought of Boston, with its maze of streets, hundreds of shops, as much a bustling city, if perhaps a bit smaller, than London.

"No, my lord, the savages do not kill at random. In fact, I come from Boston, which is a thriving city, even more so since we drove out your Redcoats."

The duke's head jerked up, his lips tightening. Lord Brandon choked on a bit of food, and the dowager duchess grinned.

"Miss Chambers, you are indeed a breath of fresh air," the dowager said, patting her lips with a serviette. "I shall enjoy meals all the more in the days to come."

"When you are through entertaining my family, perhaps you will join me in the library?" The duke addressed Merry as he stood, and then turned on his heel, not waiting for her reply.

Indeed, why would he wait for my response?

Merry decided to eat her breakfast as slowly as possible.

* * *

Kitty's gaze followed her son as he left the room. Yes, the young woman definitely affected him. For years she'd watched him view the world from his self-imposed tower. Women had fallen at his feet practically since he was out of leading strings. He'd treated them all the same. With respect, and a bit of condensation. The mamas of unmarried *ton* daughters chased him down shamelessly, which resulted in his avoidance of London during the Season.

She noted Miss Chambers and Lord Brandon as they conversed about horses, which apparently Miss Chambers was quite knowledgeable about. The girl was very pretty. Soft blond curls resting against her face brought creaminess to her skin. A light blush on her cheeks and full red lips gave her just enough color. Her son could certainly do a lot worse.

Once Lady Eleanor had surprised them all, and accepted Bedford years ago, Penrose had taken himself off the market, and named Lord Brandon as his heir. Kitty was never sure if Penrose's feelings were so engaged, or his pride merely stung. Her son didn't like to lose. And when he'd told her younger son he expected him to marry and produce the heirs to the dukedom, Kitty had been enraged.

As much as she loved both her offspring, Brandon did not possess a single attribute to be a duke. Penrose was born and bred into the role, and only *his* son would be an acceptable heir. But her stubborn eldest refused to listen to reason, and instead attempted to make Brandon into the sort of man he could never be. This American woman might very well be his unknown salvation, and Kitty's dream come true.

Penrose needed to be shaken up, challenged. Everyone deferred to him, did his bidding without thought. As lovely as Lady Eleanor had been, she would never have been an acceptable mate for him. Too blasé and conciliatory, he would have despised her weakness after a few years.

But this woman, who apparently had a mind of her own, would have him dancing to her tune. Not right away, of course. Arrogance was too deeply bred in her son for a sudden change. But change he would.

"We shall arrange for a mount while you are visiting us." Brandon wiped his mouth and leaned back in his chair.

"Oh, thank you, but I need to spend my time here with the girls."

"The duke has hired another governess, I understand, which should leave you with quite a bit of free time."

"I certainly appreciate the offer, Lord Brandon, but if I'm to help the girls with the transition to a new governess, I won't have time for much else."

He shrugged. "Nonsense. Even though my older brother is an ogre, I doubt even he would object to you taking a half hour or so to ride. We shall plan to venture out each morning before breakfast. Certainly he doesn't expect you to begin your duties at the crack of dawn."

"If I am able to obtain his permission, I will be more than happy to accompany you on a ride."

Kitty regarded them with pursed lips.

* * *

Penrose strode back and forth in front of the fireplace, his anger growing. Where the devil was the woman? All she had on her plate was a piece of toast. How long did it take to eat that? He checked his timepiece again. Almost twenty-five minutes since he left the breakfast room with instructions for her to attend him in the library.

Just as he moved to ring the bell to have a servant summon her, the door opened and Miss Chambers floated in like a queen ready to address her subjects. However did an American develop the haughtiness the aristocracy took generations of breeding to achieve?

Her blue and white striped morning gown hugged her figure a little too well for his taste. Although he had to admit she presented an inviting picture, he knew the minute she opened her mouth, the image would shatter like so much broken glass.

"Miss Chambers. Please take a seat." He motioned to

one of the chairs in front of the fireplace, and sat across from her.

She smoothed her skirts over her plump derrière and sat. Fascinated at the movement, he didn't realize he stared until she addressed him.

"Your Grace?"

What was the matter with him? He mentally shook himself and cleared his throat. "I think it would do us well to outline your duties regarding my wards so there is no confusion when the new governess arrives."

She dipped her head slightly.

Expecting an argument of sorts, he found himself at a loss as to how to go on. He jumped up and leaned an elbow on the fireplace mantle. "Miss Sarah Jennings will arrive today. She will take over the duties you've held until now. The girls need to be instructed in appropriate decorum, how to conduct themselves in Society, and the proper forms of address."

He clasped his hands behind his back, and staring at the carpet, paced in front of her. "It's obvious their education to this point has been seriously lacking. Why Lord and Lady Bedford saw fit to allow such behavior on the part of their daughters will always remain a mystery to me. However, that will end today…" He glanced at Miss Chambers, who had risen from her seat, hands fisted at her sides, her face flushed a bright red.

"How dare you!"

Penrose stiffened his shoulders, his eyes wide. "I beg your pardon."

"You should. Beg my pardon, that is." She rested her hands on her hips. "You are the most pompous man I have ever met."

"Madam, please remember to whom you are speaking."

"Excuse me? I know precisely to whom I am speaking. Lord and Lady Bedford understood the importance of a happy childhood for their daughters. They allowed them freedom, the opportunity to be little children." She raised her chin. "Despite what you think of me, I do know the importance of the station Lady Charlotte and Lady Clare were born into.

"Despite your obvious disdain for Americans, we do have manners, and treat *all* people with respect. Not just a chosen few who demand respect for no other reason than the circumstances of their birth."

She took a deep breath, obviously attempting to gain control. Her voice softened. "I also understand they will need to be taught how to conduct themselves. And, perhaps with my limited knowledge of your world, *Your Grace*, I am indeed not the best person to continue with governess duties. But I will not allow you to malign their wonderful parents who loved their girls very much, and wanted the best for them."

As if all the air in her let out, she collapsed into a chair in front of the fireplace, and touched the corner of her eyes with her knuckle.

Is she crying?

Penrose returned to his seat behind the desk, allowing Miss Chambers time to compose herself. After a minute or two, she rose and joined him. The tip of her nose was bright red, as were her cheeks. Tears clumped on her eyelashes. She looked barely older than her charges. "Please excuse my outburst."

He raised his eyebrows. The last thing he expected from her was an apology. Deciding to be gracious, he bowed his head. "I fail to understand Lord and Lady Bedford's reasoning, but I didn't mean to distress you. If I did, then I also apologize."

A slight smile tilted her lips. "You say that as though you seldom offer apologies."

"I rarely find it necessary to do so." He smiled back at her, annoyed that her smile lit up her countenance so, turning a pretty face into a beautiful one. Small lines at the edges of her eyes crinkled, making him wonder at her age.

Obviously out of the school room for years, he couldn't help but dwell on her lack of a husband.

Although he found her brash and outspoken, her beauty and feminine curves had definitely caught his attention. And that little bit of vulnerability when she cried over her employers had touched his heart. The heart he'd had under lock and key for years now, ever since Lady Eleanor had spurned his suit and chose Bedford as her husband.

He and Bedford had both danced attendance on the young debutante for the Season. She'd been named an Incomparable that year, and no one was more surprised than him when she decided on an earl instead of a duke. In retrospective, he often wondered how they would have gone on, had they married. Certainly her strange ideas on raising her daughters would have become a point of contention between them. But then, it would have been his decision in the end, anyway.

A knock at the door drew both their attentions.

A footman stood in the doorway. "Your Grace, Miss Sarah Jennings has arrived. Shall I send her in?"

Penrose glanced at Miss Chambers. "The new governess. I would prefer to speak with her alone, at first. If you would please leave us, and wait in the drawing room, I will summon you when needed."

A bright smile lit up her face. "An apology and *please* all in the same morning. This must be a record for you, Your Grace." She dipped into a slight curtsy and left the room just as the new governess entered.

CHAPTER THREE

Penrose eyed the woman the footman ushered in. He nodded in approval. Here was someone, who by her presentation alone, would be much better for Lord Bedford's daughters than the vixen who'd arrived with them.

Definitely of an age considered 'on the shelf,' Miss Jennings marched into the room, her spine as stiff as a board. Her high buttoned gown, severe knot, and no nonsense attitude reassured him of the agency's choice. He couldn't imagine for one minute this woman allowing her charges to sit on the floor in the presence of a duke.

"Your Grace," she curtsied gracefully.

"Miss Jennings," he nodded. "Please take a seat."

Penrose picked up the paper in front of him and perused it. "You come with high recommendations."

"Thank you, Your Grace."

He leaned back, and cupped his chin with his thumb and index finger, resting his elbow on the arm of the chair. "Your charges are my wards, Lady Charlotte Spencer and Lady Clare Spencer. They are the daughters of Lord and Lady Bedford, who passed away recently. The girls are twelve and nine years of age."

She nodded.

He pushed his chair back and stood.

"I'm afraid the young ladies have not been schooled in proper etiquette or demeanor thus far. I would say your arrival is most timely." He crossed his arms over his chest and regarded her. "The woman who has been their governess for the past five years is an American."

Miss Jennings sniffed.

"My thoughts exactly. Lord Bedford was my close friend, but for a strange reason, he and Lady Bedford allowed their daughters to run amok, with Miss Chambers—their present governess—the leader."

Miss Jennings tsked.

"I expect you to school the girls in feminine pursuits, preparing for their station in life, and eventual marriage to a peer. At the present time the girls are only prepared to marry a chimney sweep."

Miss Jennings shook her head, her lips pursed.

Penrose returned to his seat. "I have agreed to allow their present governess to remain, for a brief time, in order to help my wards adjust to their new surroundings." He leaned forward. "However, I wish to make it perfectly clear that you are to supervise their daily routine, and Miss Chambers is to hold no further influence over them."

Miss Jennings inclined her head in acquiescence.

"Do you have any questions?"

"None, Your Grace. I will take charge immediately so the poor young dears can start on the correct path."

The duke nodded. "Then I will ring for someone to show you to your room." He crossed the room and rang for a servant.

Miss Jennings stood as a young maid entered.

"Escort Miss Jennings to the governess's room. If Miss Chambers has not yet been relocated elsewhere, do so immediately. Also, Miss Chambers awaits me in the drawing room. Tell her I am ready to see her."

The girl bobbed. "Yes, Your Grace." She addressed

Miss Jennings. "If you will follow me, miss, I'll accompany you to the nursery."

Miss Jennings turned to the duke. "Your Grace, I am pleased to be here, and sure we can undo whatever damage the American has done to the poor little girls." Two bright spots rose on her cheeks, and her long nose twitched. Straightening her already stiff shoulders, she exited the room.

Penrose moved to a chair in front of the blazing fireplace, waiting for Miss Chambers. After several minutes, a footman entered the room.

"Your Grace, the downstairs maid indicated you wished to receive Miss Chambers. However, she is not in the drawing room."

"Not there?" Where the devil did she hie off to now? He distinctly told her to wait there to be summoned. "Have you any idea where she is?"

"Cook said she went out the back door a bit ago, with the young ladies, and appeared to be heading to the gardens."

The duke frowned, his jaw tightening. "Thank you. That will be all."

The woman dared to defy him again? He slammed his chair back and strode from the room. This situation would not continue. His long legs ate up the distance through the house and out the back door to the garden. Cook jumped in surprise when he sailed past, not having seen him in the kitchen since he'd outgrown his short pants.

Off in the distance, Miss Chambers, Lady Charlotte and Lady Clare strolled along, hand in hand. They chatted, livelier than he'd seen them until now. Just the sight of her meandering along, without a care in the world, had his heart thumping. They stopped and examined one of his mother's prized Winter Jasmine plants. Miss Chambers pointed excitedly as she spoke to the girls.

"Miss Chambers." The voice that had caused grown men to shake in their boots reached the wanderers. All three turned. Their joyful expressions collapsed.

"Did I not tell you to await my summons in the drawing room?"

"How pleasant to see you in the gardens, Your Grace. Perhaps you would like to wish a good morning to your wards?"

Penrose jerked at the distinct reprimand in her voice. Good God, the woman had audacity. To think she'd taken him to task. He opened his mouth with a rejoinder, and glanced at the two girls clinging to Miss Chamber's skirts. The younger one slipped her thumb in her mouth. Both looked up at him, eyes wide in terror.

This would not do. The woman caused him to upset the girls again. Drawing in a deep breath, he attempted to put a smile on his face. "Good morning, Lady Charlotte, Lady Clare."

"Answer His Grace," Miss Chambers urged.

They buried their faces deeper. Helplessly, he glanced at Miss Chambers, who regarded him with raised eyebrows. His blood pounded through his body, no doubt a precursor to the apoplexy she would soon cause him.

"Miss Chambers," he began.

"Yes, Your Grace." She smiled at him as if in possession of a great secret.

"Miss Jennings, the new governess will now be in charge of the young ladies' daily routine. I demand, no, *request,* you to escort them to the nursery so they may make her acquaintance."

"Very good, Your Grace." She smirked and turned the girls toward the house.

What the devil did that mean? Was she obeying his command, or complimenting him on his wording? If he didn't get Miss Chambers out of his house soon, he would be a candidate for Bedlam.

Penrose inhaled deeply to recover his control as he watched them return to the house. Miss Chamber's hips swayed gracefully beneath her pelisse, causing a different type of roaring blood to race through him. The creamy skin of her elegant neck begged to be kissed and nibbled. Wisps of golden hair teased her shoulders, released from the not-so-neat topknot. Even if his body recognized a beautiful, sensual woman, his mind put an immediate stop to that nonsense. The sooner she packed her bags and left, the better for his frame of mind. He shook his leg to adjust his breeches and followed them.

* * *

The Dowager Duchess of Penrose greeted Merry as she started up the massive staircase with the girls. "Miss Chambers. When the young ladies are settled, may I have a word with you, please?"

Merry curtsied. "Of course, Your Grace."

"Excellent. I will be in the morning room. You may ask any of the staff to direct you."

What was that all about?

If she hadn't witnessed the dowager's pleased expression and mirth-filled eyes, she would expect another dressing down. Whatever Her Grace had to say, it didn't appear to be of an unpleasant nature.

She and the girls chatted as they ascended the stairs and headed down the corridor. A patterned Brussels carpet underfoot silenced their journey. They passed through the main part of the house, and climbed another flight of stairs to where the nursery rooms were located. The girls grew quiet as they approached the end of the corridor.

Once more she had to almost drag them into the room to meet the new governess. Merry's heart bled for her charges. Prior to the carriage accident that had taken their parents so abruptly, they'd both been happy, lively young girls. After the tragedy, Merry comforted them, sang them to sleep, and held them when they sobbed. They had just reached a point where their normal exuberance for life had returned when the summons from the duke arrived, and the girls were yet again thrown into chaos.

Now they would be forced to accept a new

governess, who from the look of her, had all the softness and warmth of an iceberg. Miss Jennings stood erect, hands cupped together in front of her body as if she stood on a stage about to sing an aria. Her lips were pursed in disapproval, and her hair so tight it pulled her eyes back, giving her an oriental appearance.

The governess eyed the two girls, but her stare displayed a strong censure for Merry. Her dislike was palpable. Goodness, what had the duke told her that caused the woman to dislike her so upon sight?

"Miss Jennings?" Merry smiled, attempting to make this easier for her charges. Her stomach muscles clenched. Wrong. No longer her charges.

Miss Jennings inclined her head.

Merry decided not to extend her hand since the woman would probably view it as a breach of manners. "It's a pleasure to meet you."

"Indeed."

The governess's gaze scanned Merry from the top of her head to her shoes, tightening her lips all the while.

Merry felt her face flush. Who was this woman to judge her? Drawing herself up, Merry said, "May I introduce you to Lady Charlotte and Lady Clare."

Both girls peered at Miss Jennings from Merry's skirts.

"They are a bit overwrought at the moment. All the changes."

Under Miss Jennings' relentless gaze, Merry's anger grew. "Perhaps if you read them a story to start, it would ease them a bit."

Much to Merry's amazement, Miss Jennings walked up to the girls and bent. "Would you like to hear a story? I see His Grace has plenty of books to choose from."

"May Miss Merry read it to us?" Charlotte mumbled.

Miss Jennings smiled tightly. "Of course. Why don't you both pick a book from the shelf, and Miss Merry and I will join you at the table."

The girls released their grip and hurried to the bookcase. Miss Jennings turned to her. "Perhaps it would be of assistance if you read them a story. It's important for them to adjust to my direction since His Grace wishes to make the transition quickly and smoothly."

Merry nodded, the pain at losing her girls tugging at her. If she had not argued with the duke, perhaps he would have allowed her to remain their governess. But then she remembered he mentioned having engaged a new governess before she'd had a chance to even meet him. She sighed and wandered to the table, then pulled out one of the child-sized chairs and sat.

Two stories turned into four, but eventually the girls seemed to relax enough to allow Merry to leave them in Miss Jennings's care. Merry assured them she would be in the house, and would join them for luncheon.

The young maid she summoned escorted her to the morning room. The dowager sat behind an escritoire, a stack of pressed paper at her elbow. The soft ticking of a delicate white and blue china clock on the corner of the desk was the only sound in the room.

As Merry entered, the dowager put her quill pen down and smiled. "Thank you so much for joining me, Miss Chambers."

Merry curtsied. Her Grace caused her to feel welcome, so unlike the duke, who made no secret he could hardly await her departure.

"Please, have a seat." The dowager indicated a chair near the fireplace, where a low table held a teapot, flowered cups and saucers, and a plate of biscuits. Rising gracefully, she left her desk and joined Merry. The bright sunlight reflected off the rings on the woman's fingers as she poured tea. "Milk and sugar?"

"Yes, please." Merry studied her, wondering the reason for this meeting. The woman was as cordial as she was graceful. Her startling blue eyes looked out from a face that had seen a few years, but still remained youthful in its expression. Her dark brown hair, sprinkled with gray, gave her countenance a mature loveliness.

The dowager sipped her tea, and closed her eyes, relishing the bracing liquid. "No doubt you wonder why I asked to see you."

"Yes, Your Grace."

The older woman leaned forward, placing her cup on the table. "I'm sure you've discovered by now that my son, the duke, is a bit pompous."

Merry choked on her tea, and coughed until tears ran down her cheeks. Of all the things she'd imagined the dowager would begin the conversation with, this was not one of them.

"Well, Your Grace, he is a duke." She patted her mouth with a snowy serviette and set it alongside her cup.

The dowager gestured with her hand. "Nonsense. His father was the same way. Always thinking everyone should fall at his feet and tremble with fear at his mere presence." She glanced at Merry and smiled. "It took me a few years, but I brought him around." Looking off into the distance, she mused. "Life among the *ton* can be difficult. My husband and I had an arranged marriage. I must admit, at the beginning he did frighten me. I was a young girl, barely out of the schoolroom, and he was Penrose's age now, four and thirty."

The dowager brought her attention back to Merry. "We eventually fell in love. He was such a handsome man. Penrose takes after his father with the swarthy skin, dark hair, and deep brown eyes. I was the envy of so many of the young girls that year. He was considered quite the catch, you know.

"Our two sons were our greatest joy, and I was unfashionable enough to want to spend time with them. When they were young, my husband would roll on the floor with the boys, playing games and being silly. But, when Penrose reached an age where his father felt it was time to train him for his station in life, all the games and fun ceased."

She sighed. "I'm afraid the late duke did too good of a job. Penrose has become much too stiff. He needs to be shaken up a bit."

Merry listened, unsure of the woman's intentions in relating this story.

"No doubt you're wondering why I'm speaking thusly." The dowager seemed to read her mind. "I think you bring a breath of fresh air to Penrose Hall. I'm not happy that my son wishes to send you on your way. I also think the girls would feel much more comfortable with you in residence."

The woman certainly had her attention now. Her heart sped up in anticipation of what would come next. "What are you saying, Your Grace?"

"Why, I want you to remain with us." She raised her hand when Merry opened her mouth to speak. "Not as charity, of course. What I am asking is if you would consider accepting a position as my companion."

Merry's smile grew as she considered the idea. To be near the girls, continue to watch them grow into women. Something that up until a few minutes ago, seemed far beyond her reach. To not have the need to seek another position, possibly not as satisfying as this one had been. Then her stomach clenched, and a cloud passed overhead. *The duke.*

"While the situation you offer is most appealing, I doubt very much that His Grace would approve."

The dowager raised her chin. "I make the decisions as to whatever staff I chose to engage. I retain my own funds, so Penrose has no say in how I spend it. If I wish to employ you as my companion, then that's precisely what I shall do.

"Think," she urged, "you will see the girls daily. It will be so much easier for them to adjust to the life my son is preparing them for with you nearby. I have not met this Miss Jennings, but knowing Penrose as I do, I can well imagine what she is like."

Merry didn't answer, but smiled her agreement. "I would be honored to act as your companion, Your Grace."

"Then, if you accept, it is settled." The dowager rose and moved to the bell cord. After a few minutes, a footman appeared and bowed.

"Maxwell, please see that Miss Chamber's things are moved from the nursery wing and placed in the room across the hall from my apartments."

The dowager returned to the chair and picked up her tea cup. "We will have such good times."

Merry smiled. "I hope so, Your Grace."

"From now on, you must call me Kitty. It is how my family and friends address me, and I hope you and I will be friends." The glint in her eyes said a great deal more than Merry was comfortable with.

CHAPTER FOUR

That afternoon, after returning from a visit to a tenant, Penrose drew on the reins of his horse, Tafoya, and rested his hands on his thighs as he observed his estate. Being up high like this, above his land, always gave him a sense of flying, of freedom. The weight of his title rested heavily on his shoulders today, more so than usual. Many times over the years he had wanted to throw it all off, and like his brother, just go about enjoying life with no accountability, no restrictions.

Now he had the added responsibility of two young girls who needed guidance into womanhood. He had no doubt Miss Jennings would see to their training, but he needed to encourage his mother to take them under her wing as well, to provide the gentle hand all young girls needed. It was certainly unfortunate that Miss Chambers was such a poor influence on them. The children certainly seemed attached to her.

His chest tightened. Never in his life had he met a woman who'd gotten under his skin as the American did. Women were supposed to be soft, gentle, and defer to men's wishes and commands. In return, ladies received security and protection from men. Those tenets had been drilled into him since childhood. Then along came Miss Chambers with her soft, sensual body, creamy skin, and outlandish impertinence.

When she left the garden earlier, those plump lips smiling at what he thought was a joke on him, he wanted to snatch her back and kiss her senseless. Show her who was in charge, run his hands over those delicious curves.

He brought himself up sharp. It appeared Miss Chamber's quick departure would be best for more than one reason.

Reluctantly, he returned to the stable, his time of freedom behind him. His steward was to meet with him, and then his solicitor had sent word there were papers he still needed to sign to present to the court for the girls' guardianship.

His heart warmed at the sight of Penrose Hall rising before him as he approached from the winding path. Built from stone over one hundred years before, the home he loved always bolstered his spirits when he returned. Now with the sun dipping below the slate roof, an ethereal glow surrounded it, creating even more of a welcome.

"Good afternoon, Your Grace." Ballard, the stable master, tugged on his forelock as Penrose dismounted.

He nodded at the man. "Tafoya needs more exercise. Have him ready for me in the morning—say seven o'clock. I'm going to try to work in a ride each day."

"Will ye be joining the others, then?"

Penrose frowned. "What others?"

"Yore brother and the new lady."

"Lord Brandon is planning on riding in the mornings?" Penrose smiled and shook his head as he turned to head to the house. His younger brother rarely saw the light of day before noon. He came to an abrupt halt as the rest of the man's words penetrated his brain. "What lady?"

Ballard yanked the saddle off the horse. "That new one what's come with the little girls."

"Miss Chambers?"

"If that's her name. Don't think yore brother said."

Penrose strode away. Why would the governess be going for rides in the morning with Brandon? Of course with Miss Jennings taking over the girls' schedule, Miss Chambers would have time for a ride. Even with that justification, a sense of foreboding swept over him. She should be furiously writing letters to secure a new position. He needs remind her that her tenure here would soon come to an end.

"Have my brother join me in the library." Penrose tugged off his gloves and handed them to the footman at the door.

He crossed to a side table and poured brandy into a crystal glass. Swirling the amber liquid, Penrose settled behind his desk, noting he only had about fifteen minutes until his steward arrived for their meeting.

"I hear I've been summoned by The Duke." Brandon sauntered into the library with the perennial smirk on his face and headed directly for the brandy.

Penrose waited until his brother lounged in the chair in front of his desk, glass in hand, before he spoke. "I understand you have decided to take early morning rides."

Brandon's eyebrows rose. "I'm flattered my comings and goings are of such interest to someone as overburdened as Your Grace."

Choosing to ignore the sarcasm, Penrose took a swallow of his drink. "I'm interested enough to wonder about the identity of the young lady accompanying you."

"Ah, Ballard has been talking again." Brandon stretched out his long legs. "Give over, Penrose, you already know it's Miss Chambers, so why the games?"

"I merely wish to warn you, Miss Chambers is a governess. A temporary one at that."

"Surely you don't begrudge the woman a mount?" Brandon crossed a booted foot over his other knee, swallowing the last of his brandy. He set the glass on the desk, disregarding Penrose's frown at the wet spot under the goblet. "As for her being short-lived, I suggest you seek out Mother for enlightenment." Brandon smirked and stood, then bowing slightly, quit the room.

Mother?

Unable to spare any more time to the mystery, Penrose retrieved ledgers from the bottom shelf of the bookcase, then flipped through the pages as he waited for his steward.

* * *

"But Miss Merry always lets us go for a walk in the afternoon. She says it is part of our education." Charlotte stood with her back straight, arms crossed over her chest, a mulish expression on her face.

"Miss Chambers is no longer your governess. We will abide by my schedule which does not allow for strolls outdoors during regular schoolroom time." Miss Jennings raised her chin a notch, her face red.

"Lady Charlotte!" Merry entered the nursery in the midst of an apparent mutiny by her former charges.

Both girls hurried to her side, hugging her fiercely.

"Miss Jennings doesn't do things the right way. She won't let us go for a walk." Clare gazed up at Merry, tears rimming her eyes. She stuck her thumb in her mouth and rested her head along Merry's hip.

"Miss Jennings is now your governess, and she will surely do things differently, pet." She ran her fingers through the young girl's silky curls. "But it's part of your growth, and journey toward womanhood, to be exposed to other routines." She bent and eyed Charlotte. "And I believe you owe Miss Jennings an apology for the way you spoke to her just now."

The governess moved forward, lips in a thin line. "Thank you Miss Chambers, but I am capable of handling my charges." She turned her attention to the girls, still clinging to Merry. "Ladies, you will write a composition on proper manners. I will expect to see the finished essay before dinner."

Heat flooded Merry's face at the dismissal. Was the woman purposely attempting to make Merry dislike her? Or was it just her nature to be so abrupt? Someone else besides the girls needed to do an essay on proper manners.

At a nudge from Merry, Charlotte mumbled "Please accept my apology, Miss Jennings." The girls released Merry and trudged toward the table.

"Miss Chambers, may I speak with you outside, please?"

Merry gave her a curt nod and spun on her heel to leave the room. She waited on the other side of the doorway for Miss Jennings.

"I understand the young ladies have an attachment to you, however, now that I am in charge, I would appreciate you only coming to the nursery upon invitation. Perhaps you may join them for their afternoon tea each day."

All manner of insulting words raced through Merry's head, but realizing Miss Jennings only spoke the truth, albeit in a not very nice way, she merely nodded. "I apologize for disturbing you. I shall return for afternoon tea."

"Not today," Miss Jennings said.

Merry raised her eyebrows, afraid to open her mouth, less her vicious thoughts spew forth.

"They are being punished for poor manners. Although, I don't expect their manners to improve until they've had good *English* lessons on deportment."

After a moment of stunned silence at the woman's impudence, Merry asked, "Do you speak German, Miss Jennings?"

The woman's eyes widened. "No, I do not. Every properly brought up young lady should know French and Italian. It is not necessary for one to acquire knowledge of the more advanced languages."

"Good. *Wünsche ein tausend Floh zum ihrem Bett kommen.*"

Leaving the confused governess not understanding Merry just wished her a thousand fleas in her bed, Merry hurried away from the nursery, taking gulps of air to control her anger.

She charged down the stairs, muttering to herself until she reached the bottom of the staircase, swung left, and walked into a brick wall.

Penrose grasped her by the arms to keep her from falling backwards. Merry yelped and tried to retreat, but he held her firm.

"Are you all right, Miss Chambers?"

She looked into those deep brown eyes, now full of concern. The hint of Bay rum and brandy drifted toward her. Plus another scent that she'd already identified as Penrose. Merry struggled to contain her emotions, and replied in a shaky voice, "I am perfectly well, thank you, Your Grace."

He released her, still watching her with a guarded expression. With trembling fingers, she patted the sides and back of her hair, barely noticing it had almost fallen completely down again.

"You don't look well. Your face is flushed, and your breathing is quite rapid."

"I just came down the stairs too fast. If you will excuse me." She shifted to go around him, but he stepped into her path.

"It's more than you hurrying. Something has upset you."

Reconciled to having this conversation, Merry drew back and crossed her arms, still shaken from her encounter with Miss Jennings. "I'm afraid my attachment to the girls is stronger than I realized."

Then to her abject horror, she burst into tears.

Penrose placed his hand on her lower back and moved her toward the library. "Send some tea in, Jasper." The footman standing at the door nodded and headed in the direction of the kitchen.

The duke drew a handkerchief from his pocket and handed it to Merry. He led her to a comfortable chair in front of the fireplace where she sobbed into the cloth. The anger and embarrassment of Miss Jennings' set-down was nothing compared to the complete humiliation of succumbing to female hysterics before the duke. Sobbing like a school girl, she cried for her dear friends who'd died too young, for the beautiful daughters they left behind, and for the sadness in the girls eyes when she left them at the nursery just now.

After a few minutes, her sobs turned to soft hiccups, as a tea tray was carried in and placed on the table before her. The duke, who sat in the chair across, eyed her carefully.

She peeked at him over the handkerchief wondering if she could run from the room without making a complete cake of herself.

"No, don't leave. Have your tea, it will calm your nerves." His deep voice, kinder than she'd heard thus far, soothed her, and then immediately put her on guard.

The man was a mind reader, or was it so easy to discern her thoughts? Merry took a deep breath and cleared her throat. "I apologize, Your Grace, for that outburst."

He abruptly nodded and glanced at the teapot. Merry attempted to pour, but her shaking hands spilled the hot liquid over the tray. Penrose stilled her hand with his warm one, and took the teapot from her, pouring for both of them. "Milk and sugar?"

"Yes, please. Two lumps." Her voice came out stuffy from crying. She must look a mess. With her fair skin, red blotches generally appeared on her face when she cried. Once again she attempted to smooth her hair, but gave up. She reached for her tea, and immediately felt calmer when the warm liquid slid down her throat. One thing the English had over the Americans, and that was their belief in the restorative powers of a cup of tea.

* * *

Penrose studied the woman alongside him. Despite her disheveled appearance, he was once again struck by her beauty. Tears gathered on her full eyelashes, giving her a waiflike look. Every once in a while, she took a shuddering breath, still attempting to get herself under control. White even teeth chewed on her lower lip. Lips he would love to cover with his own, then slide his tongue along the seam until she opened, allowing him to plunder the depths of her warm, sweet mouth.

What the devil is wrong with me? The woman is a termagant, and will, thankfully, be gone very soon.

"Perhaps you can visit with the young ladies more often until both they and you are ready to go your separate ways."

Miss Chambers shook her head sadly. "Miss Jennings has set a new schedule, and I'm afraid their time with me is quite limited."

"I shall speak with her. It will certainly benefit Lady Charlotte and Lady Clare to have an easy, smooth transition."

She reached out and touched his hand, then drew it back as if burned. "I prefer you do not, Your Grace. I don't wish to cause problems."

His skin tingled where her fingers had rested. Before he had time to consider that, a light tap on the partially opened door caught his attention.

"There you are. I wanted to speak with you, but since Miss Chambers is here as well, I can talk to you both at the same time."

Penrose stood and waved his mother to his seat.

"Tea?" Miss Chambers asked.

"Yes, dear, that would be lovely."

He moved to the fireplace, resting his arm on the mantle, waiting for his mother to continue.

"With it being the beginning of December, I would like to start preparations for our Christmas Eve ball." She leaned closer to Miss Chambers. "We always have a lovely ball on Christmas Eve. We invite all the gentry in the county, and several peers who are within driving distance. It's such fun. The decorations are a huge undertaking, but I engage a few of the tenants' sons to accompany our footmen to gather greens and berries. Then their wives and daughters supply baked goods from ingredients made available to them. Some of them even help in the kitchen. But, Cook is very fussy as to whom she lets into her domain." The dowager laughed, her eyes sparkling with excitement.

"That sounds lovely." Miss Chambers' blotches had faded, but now a flush of excitement decorated her cheeks.

"I don't wish to dampen your spirits, Mother, but Miss Chambers will most likely be at her new post by Christmas."

His mother's eyes gaze slid from Miss Chambers to him. "No, dear. Miss Chambers will definitely be here for the Christmas Eve ball."

Penrose raised his eyebrows. "Indeed? Am I mistaken that Christmas is more than four weeks away? Surely you don't think it would take Miss Chambers longer than that to secure a new post?"

"Of course not. Miss Chambers already has already accepted a new situation."

His gaze swung to the governess. "You already have a new position?'

"Yes, indeed," the dowager beamed. "I've hired Miss Chambers—Merry as she's asked me to call her—as my companion."

His jaw tightened as he glared at Miss Chambers who shrugged and tilted her lips in a slight smile.

The devil take it!

CHAPTER FIVE

Merry entered the drawing room to the sound of Miss Jennings, tittering. Everyone had already gathered to await the dinner announcement.

"Miss Chambers, would you care for a sherry before dinner?" Lord Brandon sauntered over to her. Dinner hadn't even started, yet it was apparent he was already in his cups. Bloodshot eyes and a slight hesitation in his gait told the story.

"Thank you, no, my lord."

Miss Jennings let out with another giggle at something the duke said. Merry glanced in her direction and swallowed a laugh. The woman wore a pink gown more suited to a young miss. Rosy cheeks on her otherwise sallow complexion grew as she flirted—there was no other word—with Penrose.

Heavens, where was the very proper governess who'd disparaged her? Merry's gaze moved from the pink nightmare to His Grace. Her heart almost stopped. No man should be that handsome. His dark brown eyes above a strong jaw almost had her giggling like Miss Jennings. No padding had been necessary in the jacket that fit him like a glove, and his snug breeches outlined the taut muscles of his legs.

"They make quite a pair." Lord Brandon leaned close to her ear, his brandy-laced breath wafting over her.

Merry started at his words, then chastised herself for staring. "Whatever do you mean?"

Lord Brandon smirked and sipped his drink. "I think Miss Jennings has her eye on my big brother. Although, with you in the room, I don't see how the poor woman has a chance."

Heat rose from her middle and shot up to her face. Scanning the room for something else to comment on to calm herself, she caught His Grace staring at her, his look so intent she thought perhaps she'd forgotten to put on her gown. Her face grew hotter.

"Excuse me. There is something I must discuss with your mother." She hurried away from Lord Brandon, the sound of his chuckle in her ear. Before she reached Kitty, speaking animatedly with a middle aged man unknown to her, one of the footmen announced dinner.

"Here she is now, Lord Moreland." Kitty took the arm of the man and joined Merry. "Lord Moreland, I would like to introduce you to my companion, Miss Chambers. His lordship is one of our neighbors who occasionally grants us the pleasure of his company."

"Delighted," the man said, bowing slightly.

Merry curtsied. "A pleasure, my lord."

He extended his other arm to her, and she placed her hand there, and the three sauntered into the dining room. Miss Jennings had a firm grasp on His Grace's arm, and Lord Brandon viewed them over the rim of his glass as they quit the room. He winked at her as she moved past.

Once they'd settled into their places, footmen began pouring wine and serving the soup.

"Miss Chambers, am I to assume from your accent you are American?" Lord Moreland smiled at her as he raised his wine glass to his lips.

"Yes, my lord. I am from Boston."

"Sir, I must commend you on your astuteness," Miss Jennings said. "I believe Miss Chambers has tried, although unsuccessfully, to adopt proper English speech. 'Tis a shame my young charges have picked up some of her American vernacular."

Oblivious to the stunned silence following her words, she cast a smile at the duke, who frowned, then glanced at Merry.

Is he frowning because the girls are worse off than he thought?

She swallowed her annoyance as Lord Brandon leaned toward her. "Don't let her get away with that."

Merry shook her head and spooned the delicious pheasant soup into her mouth. She would not involve herself in a war of words with the governess. At least not in front of the duke. He already held Miss Jennings in high regard, and Merry would merely come across looking churlish.

After the second course had been served, and the footmen stationed at their places against the wall should anyone require their assistance, Lord Moreland turned his attention once again to Merry. "Tell us about Boston, Miss Chambers."

Merry beamed. "Boston is a wonderful city, my lord. It has a long history, being one of the first cities settled after the colonists arrived. But now it is a bustling place, comparable to London."

"Certainly nothing in the Colonies can compare to London?" Miss Jennings' whiny voice grated on her ears.

Merry smiled at the governess. "Miss Jennings, you do remember we are no longer the Colonies? We defeated your countrymen—for the second time—a few years ago."

The duke affected a choking sound, and Lord Brandon once again leaned toward her. "Bravo, my girl."

She took a deep breath in an attempt to calm herself. This was neither the time nor place to indulge in petty bickering.

Lord Moreland saved the day. "What were some of

your favorite places in Boston?"

Relieved, she happily returned her attention to him. "I loved every part of it, my lord. I enjoyed walking to Dorchester Heights and gazing out over the sea. We also have a new Science museum, and a wonderful library for the public where I spent a great deal of time."

"You are interested in books?"

"Oh, yes. My father was a professor at Harvard."

He frowned. "What encouraged you to travel to England?"

"Lord and Lady Bedford had just lost their dear nanny. She contracted a fever while traveling in Boston and died. My father had recently passed, and I thought a change of scenery would be beneficial, so I agreed to accompany them to England as their governess."

"And how do you find England, my dear?"

"I've been here five years and grow to love it more each day." Merry's natural enthusiasm took over. "Everything is so green and lovely. I even enjoy the foggy and rainy days. When Lord and Lady Bedford were in London for the Season, I was permitted to visit the theater, museums and symphony."

"I wonder why it is that a woman as lovely as yourself has not been snatched up by some young buck?" Lord Moreland cast her a warm smile.

Merry raised her chin. "I prefer to marry for love, my lord. And thus far that has not come my way."

Miss Jennings snickered. "Miss Chambers, certainly you don't believe marriage requires love?"

"Marriage perhaps doesn't require love, but certainly makes the union more pleasant."

With a wave of her hand, Miss Jennings dismissed her. "Such an American viewpoint. Marriages are to form alliances, strengthen the bloodlines, create heirs." She smiled in her direction as if Merry were an unsophisticated child, attempting to discuss adult matters.

"I'm afraid I must agree with Miss Chambers." The

duke spoke to Miss Jennings, but his eyes never left Merry. "If one must spend the rest of one's life with a woman, why not have it be someone you care deeply for?"

"Surely you jest, Your Grace?" Miss Jennings chided, her hand at her throat. "Someone in Your Grace's position knows the duty in marriage."

A few seconds passed, and then the duke directed his attention to Miss Jennings. "Of course. Every peer knows what marriage is all about."

Miss Jennings threw a smug look at Merry.

The rest of the meal passed in pleasant conversation. The few times Merry glanced at the duke, his eyes were on her, assessing, causing her to want to squirm in her seat.

After the final course had been removed, Kitty stood. "I believe the ladies will retire to the drawing room and leave you gentlemen to your port. Ladies?" The dowager moved to the doorway, Miss Jennings and Merry in her wake.

* * *

Penrose studied the women as they left the room. His gaze drifted to Miss Chamber's slender back, then slid down to her lovely derrière and the gentle sway of her hips. He felt a tightening in his groin at the sight.

Miss Jennings might hold her counterpart in disdain, but Miss Chambers had shown more character and intelligence than three of Miss Jennings. He still thought Miss Jennings was the better governess for his wards. But his mind and body knew who he'd prefer to have underneath him in his bed, and alongside him at the dinner table.

Merry Chambers had passion. When she baited him, and when she spoke of Boston, it was there in her eyes. To unleash that passion would be a man's pleasure. But with her notions of marriage with love, it would be best to stay far away from her.

He hadn't loved Lady Eleanor all those years ago when he'd lost to Bedford. He'd merely decided she would make an excellent duchess. Her family was an old, respected one. She was graceful, charming, and beautiful. He would've had no problem bedding her, but in no way did she stir his blood. The only woman who had ever done that had just left the room.

Drat his mother for employing Miss Chambers. As delightful as she was to look at and daydream about, she still possessed those odd ideas about her station in life. She certainly had no regard for the difference in classes. She felt free to bait him whenever the mood struck her. Never had anyone, particularly a woman, stood up to him the way she did.

Perhaps her reaction *to* him came from the same fire that burned *in* him. He smiled. They certainly did seem to rile each other.

Suddenly he looked forward to having Miss Chambers about for a while. Life had become too dull and predictable.

* * *

Merry tossed in her bed, attempting to get comfortable enough to sleep. Finally realizing that comfort wasn't the problem, she threw off the quilt and swung her legs over the edge. Feeling around with her toes, she slid her feet into her slippers and grabbed the wrapper at the foot of her bed.

Perhaps if she had a book she could read until she felt sleepy. Every time she closed her eyes, a vision of Penrose, with his deep brown eyes and wicked smile, tortured her. How could a man be so comely and have such arrogance at the same time? She didn't want to be aware of his presence, his scent. Nor to think on how his large hands would feel touching her skin, or his lips closing over hers. The man was a duke for heaven's sake, and even she, an American, knew he was well beyond her.

Goodness, now I'm beginning to sound like Miss Jennings.

Merry quietly slipped out of her room and descended the stairs. The door to the library stood partially opened, but no candlelight glowed. She entered the room and inhaled deeply of the comforting smell. How she loved being surrounded by books, and the inevitable scent of brandy. The air in her father's library had always carried the same mixture.

She found a small candelabra with a flint alongside it on a table near the door. With the lighting in front of her, she headed to the bookshelves and began to peruse the titles, looking for something uninteresting enough to lull her to sleep. Her gaze wandered over volumes of history and science.

"Ah, another nighttime wanderer."

Merry yelped and jumped as that deep voice rolled over her. She spun around, the movement causing the candles to snuff out. "Your Grace, you scared me to death!"

"I apologize, Miss Chambers." He must have moved in her direction because she could sense his presence. "Here, allow me to re-light your candles."

A flash of light, and his face appeared above the flint he held. With the shadows cast upon his countenance, he looked almost sinister. He smiled, white teeth flashing, and the picture of the devil himself was complete.

Merry's mouth dried up, and she eased back, hitting the bookcase behind her. "I'm...I hoped...I was looking for a book." She ran her tongue over her lips. What sounded like a growl emanated from deep within Penrose's chest.

"Do not let me keep you from your search." He touched the flint to a candle he held in his hand and moved away. Penrose made his way to the sideboard. "I merely came for a bit of brandy to aid my sleep." Though she couldn't easily see him in the dark shadows beyond the circle of candle light blinding her, the sound of the liquid hitting the glass played over her ears.

"May I pour you some sherry?"

Her heart thumped in her chest, and not all from the

fright he'd given her. Here she stood in her nightgown, with only a flimsy wrapper over it. Instead of rushing from the room to protect her virtue, she seriously considered accepting his offer. "Yes, Your Grace."

Why in heaven's name did I say that?

"Excellent. Come join me by the fireplace, and I'll soon have a blazing fire to warm us."

She took a step, then hesitated. "I'm not really sure which way to go."

"Wait. I'll come to you."

His warm hand reached out and grasped her elbow. She drew in a sharp breath as her skin heated where he touched. After a short walk, she was relieved to reach the chair and break the contact. She took the glass of sherry from him with a shaky hand. Penrose studied her for a minute, the sharp planes of his face mimicking a drawing of the devil she'd seen as a child.

"Do you often have problems sleeping?" He settled in the chair next to her and regarded her over the rim of his brandy glass.

Now more clearly visible with the glow from the fireplace, the duke mesmerized her. He'd removed his jacket and cravat, exposing the tanned skin at his throat, wisps of dark curls peeking up from his shirt opening. A brightly colored banyan covered his white shirt and breeches. His dark hair fell over his forehead in waves, causing her fingers to twitch with the desire to smooth it back.

"Sometimes." She sipped her sherry, already feeling lightheaded, but not, she suspected, from the wine.

He swallowed a bit of the amber liquid, closing his eyes briefly as he did. She watched, fascinated, as his throat muscles worked. Her body warmed and softened, parts of her she never thought about tingled, inducing her to shift in the seat. This was preposterous. If she didn't leave soon, her body would slide to the floor in a puddle. She placed her glass on the table between them and stood. "I must be off to bed now."

"Please don't go, Miss Chambers."

Merry hesitated, but reluctantly sat. "The two of us being here together, alone, is not proper."

"You are correct, but who's to know, except us?"

"That's not the point, Your Grace. What would Miss Jennings say?"

"Ah, Miss Jennings." He slanted Merry a look. "The perfect governess."

She gave an unladylike snort. A glance at the duke caught him in a smile.

"It appears Miss Jennings does not quite approve of you."

"Neither do you, Your Grace."

His brows drew together. "Please stop with the 'Your Grace.' It gets burdensome after a while."

Merry's lips quirked. "I have the feeling you rarely find your title burdensome, Your..."

"Penrose. Why don't you call me that instead?" When she inclined her head, he remarked, "So you believe love and marriage are compatible?" His intense gaze encompassed her as if she were a bug under glass. She felt exposed and smothered at the same time.

Nonplussed by his quick shift in conversation, she raised her chin. "Yes, I do. My parents had a love match, and I will not marry without love."

"Foolish child." He shook his head as he studied the brandy he swirled.

"I beg your pardon!" Merry felt the heat rise to her face.

He glanced quickly at her. "Once again I must apologize. I meant no insult."

"Her Grace told me she and your father were in love."

"That's true. However, it didn't start that way, and they were lucky love remained. Things could turn messy if a couple fell out of love. Better to marry without that expectation." He drained the last of his brandy and set the glass aside. "To me marriage is all a business arrangement, nothing more."

"And at four and thirty you have not been successful in securing a *business arrangement* for yourself?"

"Ah. Straightforward speaking. A trait of the Americans."

Since her brash statement didn't have him ordering her to her room, she continued. "You are a duke, with responsibilities. Surely someone as dedicated to his title as you are would have ensured the continuation of the Penrose line and filled his nursery by now. An *heir and a spare*, is that not the accepted vernacular?"

"Lord Brandon is my heir."

"And it appears he has done nothing to secure the title, either. So neglectful, Your Grace."

He grinned. "You do realize how far over the line you have stepped, Miss Chambers?"

She inclined her head. "Yes, please excuse my *straightforward* speaking. I am afraid it doesn't bode as well here in England as it does in America."

"Which Americans have in abundance."

"As you say." She sighed and stood. "That little bit of sherry has rendered me drowsy. I'm sure I will be able to sleep now."

Penrose stood at the same time she did. "Alas, I find the brandy did not soothe me as much as I'd hoped."

"Perhaps a book?"

"I have a better idea." He moved toward her, and set his hands on her shoulders. "Do you know why Miss Jennings dislikes you so?"

Merry shook her head, the ability to speak having fled. Her skin burned where his warm palms held her, his strong fingers kneading her flesh. She should not allow these liberties. But it was, oh, so hard to move away from his commanding presence. His eyes held her prisoner. She moved her gaze to his sensual lips.

"Because you're a beautiful woman—Merry." He edged her closer. "Isn't that what the girls and my mother call you?"

His eyes danced with mirth and something else. Undefinable, and fleeting. Her senses were awash with his smell, touch, warmth. The dark room, lit only by the glow from the fireplace, with his strong body blocking out the darkness, enveloped her with an aura of peace and danger all at the same time. She tried desperately to remember his question. "Yes." Her voice, having recovered, decided to only whisper. "Your Grace…"

"Shh." His head descended and she closed her eyes. Before she could process what was happening, he slid his warm palm against her cheek and cupped her chin, stroking her jaw with his thumb. Tugging her lightly, he pulled her closer and took possession of her mouth. Sparks exploded behind her eyelids. Heat rushed from her belly up to her face, stopping along the way to set her heart to thundering. She slid her palms up Penrose's chest, resting her hands on his shoulders. Firm and warm.

In a quick move, he crushed her breasts against his hard chest, shifting his head, allowing him better access to slip his tongue into her mouth as she gasped. Had she not been holding firm to him, she would, indeed, have melted to the floor in a puddle of hot liquid.

After plundering her mouth, he pulled back and rested his forehead against hers, his fingers playing with the soft skin behind her ears. "As a gentleman, I should apologize, but I hope I haven't frightened you."

Merry drew her head back. "I don't frighten easily."

His hands dropped to his side. "I'm sure you don't, but perhaps in this instance you should."

She turned and fled the room, her emotions in a turmoil.

* * *

What have I just done?

Penrose slumped in his seat, his member rock hard

from the kiss he'd shared with Merry. She was everything he was afraid she'd be. Warm, soft, and passionate. Her huge blue eyes, darkened by desire, stared into his before she'd run from him. Despite her enthusiastic response to his touch, she was an innocent. And not someone he should be trifling with.

I will not marry without love.

Too bad she wasn't suitable, she would make a wonderful duchess. Proud, courageous, and graceful. He grinned. As long as she kept her mouth closed in public. But, oh, how he'd like to rile her in private, and watch all that anger turn into passion.

For him.

He stretched his long legs out and crossed his arms. Her comments about his duty stung. If he truly intended to never marry, he needed to take his brother in hand and prepare him for his role as duke should something happen to him. Brandon also needed to be encouraged to marry and fill the nursery, as Miss Chambers had so untactfully noted.

If he'd thought it a mistake to rely on Brandon when he'd first approached him about his decision not to marry, over time his brother's lack of interest in the estate confirmed his suspicions. Perhaps he should reconsider, and find a wife for himself. Someone befitting the title duchess, who already had a place in Society.

He groaned at the idea of presenting himself in London, and making the rounds of balls, musicals, and routs next Season to find a suitable bride. Giggling girls just out of the schoolroom would be dragged across the floor by their determined mamas once he appeared. Could he subject himself to several months of that?

Once more, Miss Chambers invaded his thoughts. She of the beautiful face, fine figure, and outspoken manner. He sighed and picked up the candle next to him for his trek upstairs to bed. It was best to forget about the woman. She was not the mistress type, and he would never consider marriage to someone as audacious as the former governess.

But with the state she'd left him in, perhaps it was time to make a visit to his widow friend sometime soon.

CHAPTER SIX

Early the next morning, Merry hurried to the stables to meet Lord Brandon for their outing. Having practically been raised on a horse, she was thrilled to have the chance to ride once again. Bedford Hall had an impressive stable, and she often rode when she had the chance. But amid all the upheaval with Lord and Lady Bedford's deaths, and preparations for the move to Penrose, she'd hadn't ridden in weeks.

Ballard led a dark grey mare from the stable as Lord Brandon joined her.

"Oh, what a beauty!" Merry ran her gloved hand over the magnificent horse's velvet nose. "What is her name?"

"Aphrodite, miss."

She beamed. "A perfect dub."

"Good morning, Merry. I must admit this is not my favorite time of day." Lord Brandon's drawn face and bloodshot eyes confirmed his words.

"I could ride by myself. I'm an experienced horsewoman." Her gaze roamed his face. "You do look as though you could use more sleep."

"No. It would not be a good idea for you to ride alone. You're not familiar with the land, and I would hate for something to happen to you."

"Don't concern yourself, brother, I will be more than happy to escort Miss Chambers on her ride." Dressed in the height-of-fashion riding clothes, Penrose strode toward them, pulling on tan leather gloves.

Merry's stomach clenched. The light of day only intensified his good looks. Had those full lips actually ravished hers last night? His glance at her was warm, without the hint of disapproval she'd always seen before.

Be careful. He is a duke, and you can't afford to allow your thoughts to wander in that direction.

"Miss Chambers would you mind terribly if I excuse myself?" Lord Brandon's eyes pleaded with her.

"Of course she doesn't mind. You best search out Cook for one of her tonics." The duke turned to Ballard. "Is Tafoya ready?"

Merry stood, her mouth agape, as Lord Brandon gave her a short two-finger salute and hurried to the house.

"Excuse me, Your Grace, but I would prefer to answer for myself."

He frowned at her. "What do you mean?"

"You don't even know, do you?" She shook her head. "Lord Brandon just asked me if I minded him not riding with me, and you answered."

"Do you mind him not accompanying you?" He looked genuinely confused.

"That is not the point."

His eyes flashed with annoyance. "What is the point?"

"Never mind. This conversation is a waste of words." Before he could assist her, she stepped on the block and settled on the sidesaddle, adjusting the deep blue skirts of her riding habit over her legs.

Penrose gracefully mounted his horse and took up the reins. "Are you ready? I wouldn't want to start off without asking."

Merry smirked. "Yes. I'm ready."

They rode side-by-side down the path leading from the house, neither one aware of the narrowed eyes watching them from the schoolroom window.

* * *

Despite the cold, late fall air, the sun shone in the rarely clear sky, reaffirming Penrose's decision to begin taking morning rides. Lord, he missed this. For a while he could forget his duties and just enjoy a ride with a beautiful woman at his side.

And beautiful she was. Her velvet riding habit hugged her curves delightfully. The deep blue brought out the color of her eyes, which sparkled with pleasure as she inhaled deeply, causing his attention to shift to her breasts. Just the right size for his hands, he imagined their silky softness.

"Do you ride every day, Your Grace?"

Her question drew him from his reverie. "No. In fact this is the first time I've ridden for pleasure in a while." He slanted a look at her. "I thought we agreed last night to dispense with 'Your Grace'?"

"'Tis not proper. You are my employer."

"Not so. You are employed by my mother who, as I'm sure she's told you with a great deal of satisfaction, has her own funds to do with as she wishes."

"True. But I am not of your world."

He grinned. "You sound like Miss Jennings."

"The perfect governess?" Her eyebrows rose, one side of her mouth tilted.

Ready to take umbrage at her remark, instead he threw his head back and laughed. "Miss Jennings may be aware of your position in life, but I believe you are not."

She bristled. "I understand your class structure, I'm no fool. However, as I was not raised with all the nuances your way clings to, and being from America where one is judged by what one does, not by one's birth, I find it hard to swallow."

"Ah yes, the American method. Anyone of ability

may rise to the top."

Merry drew her shoulders back. "And a fine system it is."

He grinned. "As you say."

God, how he loved baiting her. She was all spit and fire. Right now her eyes flashed and two bright red spots appeared on her cheeks. Her chest heaved, bringing his attention once again to those delectable breasts. If he didn't get himself under control soon, the ride would be a tad uncomfortable.

All the women of his acquaintance, including the young misses of the Marriage Mart he stopped visiting a few years ago, fell at his feet and agreed with everything he said. He was used to tittering, flirting, adoration, and admiring glances cast above silk fans. Merry Chambers did none of that, and he found the change refreshing. Frustrating as the devil, though. The woman did not know her place.

"Shall we give the horses their head?" Merry asked, a mischievous sparkle in her eyes.

He swept his arm out. "Lead on."

Merry took off at a gallop, almost leaving him behind. He squeezed his knees and Tafoya burst forth, soon overtaking the mare. Merry grinned as he passed her, and then urged her mount to catch up. He held Tafoya back so they could race alongside each other. The bracing air rushing past his face invigorated him, producing a sense of rightness and peace he hadn't felt in a long time.

Eventually, they slowed and brought the horses to a canter, then a trot. "That was wonderful!" Merry exclaimed.

He agreed for an entirely different reason. Her topknot had come loose, with tendrils of curls surrounding her face. The exertion of running in the cold air had put color into her face. She licked her lips and he groaned under his breath, once more wanting to cover those luscious lips with his own.

Suddenly, Aphrodite reared. Merry yelped and attempted to control the beast, but the horse bucked again, throwing her to the ground. Within seconds, the mare turned and raced back toward the stables.

Penrose jumped from his horse and hurried to where Merry sat on the ground. "Are you all right?" He squatted and studied her face.

"I think so." Merry took a deep breath. "I'm not sure what happened." She shifted to rise.

"No, don't move just yet. You've had quite a fall, and you need to be sure you didn't break anything."

She extended her arms and legs. "I don't think so. I'm actually sorer on my…. Never mind."

Penrose helped her gain her feet. When she stumbled against him, he scooped her into his arms.

She gasped, her eyes wide. "What are you doing?"

"I don't think you're in any condition to walk." He strode to his horse and lifted her to the saddle. With one quick motion he mounted behind her.

"This is most improper." She attempted to cover herself with her skirts, but they'd been twisted underneath her, exposing the bottom half of her legs.

"Don't concern yourself. We need to get you home and send for the doctor."

"Oh, for heaven's sake. I'm fine. I don't need a doctor."

"That's my decision to make." Urging his horse, they cantered forward.

Penrose tried desperately to ignore the soft body resting on his. Her lemon scent drifted to him, tempting him further. His arm burned where it wrapped around her middle, his fingers itching to ease upward and embrace a warm breast. Thankfully, the ride didn't take too long, since he feared she could feel his throbbing desire pressing against her bottom.

They entered the stable yard. Aphrodite stood panting, her mouth wet with white foam. Ballard ran his hands over her. "What happened, Your Grace?"

"Something hurt or spooked her, and she threw Miss Chambers. See if you can figure out what caused her to bolt like that. I'm taking Miss Chambers to the house."

Penrose slid off the horse and reached for her.

"I can walk."

"Not until the doctor has seen you." He settled her in his arms.

"You are being ridiculous. I know I'm not injured."

His lips tightened. "You are my responsibility. You will see the doctor."

"I am not your responsibility. Furthermore, I know if I can walk or not." She raised her voice.

"As long as you reside under my roof, you will abide by my wishes."

"You mean orders. You, sir, are an impossible man."

"I agree."

The footman opened the door at their approach, his eyebrows raised at Penrose carrying Merry, with both of them snarling at each other.

"I'm taking Miss Chambers to her room. Please send for the doctor, she's had a spill from her horse."

Merry crossed her arms over her chest. "I do not need a doctor."

"Nevertheless, he will be sent for." He started up the stairs.

"I protest."

"Excellent. You may protest in bed while you wait for the doctor."

"You may not carry me into my bedroom."

He raised his eyebrows. "Says who?"

Merry lowered her voice. "Miss Jennings."

"She is the governess. I, on the other hand, am the duke."

As they reached the top of the stairs, his mother came from her sitting room. "What in heaven's name is going on? My poor ears have been tortured with bickering from all the way outside."

"Miss Chambers took a fall from her horse. I'm taking her to her room while we wait for the doctor."

"Oh my goodness. Is she badly hurt?" The dowager hurried behind them.

"I'm not hurt at all," Merry called over his shoulder. "But His Grace is too stubborn to listen to me."

As his mother stepped in front of them to open the door, she covered her mouth with her hand, looking suspiciously as if she tried to hold back a laugh.

"The doctor will determine if you are injured or not," Penrose growled. He swung past the dowager and strode to Merry's bed where he deposited her gently.

"Dear, you must leave us now." His mother looked from him to Merry.

"Fine. Stay with her Mother, and make sure she doesn't move until the doctor sees her."

She smirked. "Yes, dear."

"I don't need a doctor," Merry called to Penrose's retreating back. He slammed her door.

* * *

Much to Merry's disgust, and even though he'd found no injuries, the doctor ordered her to stay in bed for the rest of the day. Nonsense. She felt fine, and had been thrown from a horse more than once. That arrogant, stubborn man who insisted on sending for the doctor annoyed her to no end. Why she ever thought him attractive remained a mystery.

Shortly after noontime, Kitty entered the chamber, followed by a young maid carrying a tray containing soup and bread. "I brought you the lovely soup Cook fixed for luncheon."

"You should not be waiting on me. For goodness sake everyone is acting like I'm some sort of invalid."

Kitty directed the maid to set the tray on the table next to the bed. "I'm afraid when Penrose gets something into his mind, it doesn't leave easily." She snapped open the snowy white serviette and handed it to Merry. "And I have an ulterior motive. I want to begin making the plans for the Christmas Eve ball."

"Of course. I'll be happy to take notes." Merry shifted to lean against the pillows.

"Eat your meal first, and then we can work."

The duchess talked as Merry ate the delicious thick soup and fresh bread.

"The Penrose Christmas Eve Ball has been a tradition for generations. In fact, the original ball was held the Christmas after the first King George had assumed the throne. The story is passed down that he actually attended, but there has never been anything written to prove that."

Merry laid her spoon alongside her bowl. "I am looking forward to it. Lord and Lady Bedford hosted a very small gathering on Christmas Eve each year, because they included the girls. They also had what they called a "Christmas Tree," a tradition they learned from their German cook. Several footmen cut down a pine, and they set it up in the house. They the girls would make paper dolls, stars, and such, to hang on the tree. It was quite entertaining, and brought a wonderful smell to the drawing room."

"I have heard of that. Maybe we should do the same here. I'm sure the girls will love it."

"I agree. That activity might bring a little bit of their parents back." She wiped her mouth and placed the tray away from her. "I'm finished with my soup, and ready to plan the ball."

* * *

Merry's eyes shot open at the sound of young voices. "Miss Merry! We've come to visit with you."

Apparently her sore body had needed the rest, for she had fallen asleep. Lady Charlotte and Lady Clare raced into her room, with Miss Jennings following behind. "Ladies always walk," she scolded.

"His Grace wished for the girls to call since you

won't be able to join them for afternoon tea." Miss Jennings's lip curled and she looked so far down her nose, Merry thought the governess would become permanently cross-eyed.

"Thank you very much for bringing them."

"It was His Grace's wishes." She sniffed, all her displeasure in the sound.

"What happened, Miss Merry? The duke told us you were injured in a spill from your horse."

Merry sighed. "No, pet. I was not injured. I did fall from my horse, but aside from a few aches and—mostly in the area where I sit down—I'm fine."

At Miss Jennings' sharp inhale, Merry glanced at her.

"This is not proper conversation for young girls."

Merry raised her eyebrows. "What did I say?"

Miss Jennings drew herself up. "A properly brought up lady never mentions any part of her body."

Biting back a retort, Merry returned her attention to the girls, encouraging them to tell her all about their lessons.

After about fifteen minutes of visiting, Miss Jennings reminded the girls the time drew near for their tea. Hugging Merry fiercely, they left to return to the nursery. Their governess remained behind.

Once the latch on the door caught, Miss Jennings moved closer to Merry's bed. "I know what you're trying to do."

"I beg your pardon?"

Her eyes grew to slits. "I thought you claimed to be an experienced rider?"

"And if I did?"

"Then how is it you came to *fall* from your horse?"

Merry's jaw muscles worked. The nerve of this woman! "Not that it's any of your concern, but my horse unexpectedly reared and threw me."

"Right into His Grace's arms?"

Stunned into speechlessness, Merry didn't move a

muscle as the governess hissed.

"You can forget what you're thinking. The Duke of Penrose will never stoop so low as to marry a foreigner. And from America, no less," she sneered. Pacing in front of the bed, she slapped a fist into her hand. "If he were to select a wife not a member of the *haut ton,* he would surely choose me. I'm English. My father was a member of the gentry."

Recovering her voice, Merry said, "How exceedingly pleasant for you."

"Don't condescend to me. I see the way you look at His Grace, and he may be attracted to you. But be assured, a quick tumble in his bed is all he is interested in."

Merry drew in a sharp breath at the woman's crudeness. "From what I understand, His Grace is not in the market for a wife. In fact, if you are wishing to secure a husband, I advise you to look to his brother. Lord Brandon has been named the duke's heir."

"Nonsense. No duke would ignore his duty. And Lord Brandon is sorely wanting in so many ways."

Merry thought of the young man with the sparkling wit and charming ways. The man who befriended her from the first. "Miss Jennings, you are unpleasant and rude. Please leave me."

"I will. As soon as I finish." She came to stand directly over Merry, her face in a vicious snarl. "You may have cajoled Her Grace into hiring you as a companion so you don't have to leave, but you'll never get your hands on her son. He is a duke, and you are a nobody."

Quelling the unladylike desire to rip out the governess's hair, she gave a tight smile. "Thank you for your kind words. Now please leave me in peace."

Miss Jennings patted her hair, and tugged on the sleeves of her gown. Turning on her heel, she headed to the door. She gripped the door latch and viewed Merry over her shoulder. "Just remember what I said. I can assure you if anyone in this house is to be the next

Duchess of Penrose, it will be me."

Merry blew out the breath she held. Miss Jennings was more than welcome to the duke. His arrogance was something she would never put up with.

Then she touched her lips with her fingertips. Remembering…

CHAPTER SEVEN

Penrose blew on his hands, bitingly cold, even though he wore gloves. He glanced out the window at the darkening sky. Definitely snow in the air.

The crested coach stopped in front of the Hall, and the butler had the front door open before Penrose alighted from the conveyance. He gathered up his satchel, full of papers he'd acquired on his five day trip to Lord Smithfield's estate.

Twice a year he and Lords Smithfield and Eastlake met at one of their homes to discuss bills they wished to sponsor in the Lords, and to compare notes on estate matters. When the duchy had been unexpectedly thrust upon him at a young age, the lords, who had been his father's peers and close friends, had provided him with a steady hand in the old duke's place. After years of running his own estate, Penrose now made as many helpful suggestions as the others.

As he strode to the front door, his thoughts, as had many times during his time away, drifted toward Merry. He chuckled when he remembered the morning he'd left, and how enraged she'd become when he'd sent word that she had his permission to leave her bed after her injury. She'd tore down the stairs and let him know she had every intention of being up and about and certainly did not need his permission to do so. With all that fire and wrath, he wanted nothing more than to drag her to him and conquer her mouth as he wished to conquer her body.

"Good afternoon, Your Grace." His butler, Jones, bowed. "It looks like we're in for a bit of nasty weather." He helped Penrose off with his greatcoat.

"Yes it does. Where is my mother?" The woman he really wanted to see would most likely be with her.

"I believe she and Miss Chambers are working in the dining room."

Already an air of festivity surrounded him. Girls from the village, who only came during the holidays to help out, were busy decorating the Hall. Someone had gathered greens, and their scent brought him to where his mother and Merry—*sitting on the floor at his mother's feet*—chatted and laughed.

"Penrose, you're home!" Mother rose from her chair alongside Merry and embraced him. He returned her hug, glancing over her shoulder at the vixen sitting in a most unladylike manner on the floor. His eyebrows rose.

Merry regarded him, a slight smile on her lips, her head tilted.

A challenge?

Her slender fingers brushed back the wisps of blond hair that had fallen on her forehead. A smudge of dirt dusted her cheek, and she wore an old gown with a soiled apron over it. She never looked more beautiful to him. His groin tightened, and the sight of her pitched him into the whirlwind of emotions brought on by the minx.

"Miss Chambers." He released his mother and nodded in Merry's direction.

"Your Grace." She moved to rise, and he extended his hand to help her. Despite his cool and logical mind, the jolt he felt was real. Merry jerked her hand back as if she felt it, too.

Penrose's gaze roamed the women's work area. Stacks of linens sat alongside plates, cups, saucers and chests of silver. He directed his attention to his mother. "What are you doing? It looks to me like you're preparing for a feast."

The dowager smiled brightly. "Exactly, my dear. Since you've been gone, Miss Chambers and I have been busy getting ready for the Christmas Eve ball. And the rest of the holidays, of course." She took him by the arm and headed toward the doorway. "Perhaps we could all use a respite. I'll send for refreshments."

He turned. "Will you join us, Miss Chambers?"

"Yes, thank you, Your Grace. Please excuse me while I freshen up."

His mother smiled fondly at Merry's back. "Miss Chamber has been working very hard. We've just about finished the counting of linens and dinnerware. Merry also supervised the young girls from the village since Mrs. Bond was busy with her housekeeping duties." She squeezed his arm. "Oh I do love the holidays, Penrose. We should entertain more often."

Her excitement was contagious. He found himself smiling along with her. "Would you really wish to take on all this extra work several times a year?"

She waved her hand in dismissal as they entered the drawing room. "Miss Chambers is such a help, I feel as though I'm doing nothing at all."

"But Miss Chambers may not be with us forever. Some young man may catch her fancy and she'll be off planning her own parties." His gut clenched at his own words.

His mother glanced at him, a mysterious smile on her face. "Yes. Perhaps Miss Chambers will catch the eye of a young man. Or, maybe she already has."

Penrose's heart sped up, but he kept his voice cool. "What do you mean? Have there been callers in my absence?"

The dowager sighed. "Sometimes I do wonder at your intelligence, my son." She turned to the maid she'd summoned and instructed her to fetch tea and sandwiches.

They moved further into the room, settling on the settee near the warming fireplace.

"You still have not answered my question. Has Miss Chambers been receiving callers?"

"No, my dear. No one outside the family has been to see her."

"Brandon?" He would never allow Merry to seriously consider his brother. As much as he loved the younger man, he had quite a bit of growing up to do before he took on a wife. Although, as the heir apparent to the dukedom, he should be encouraging Brandon to marry. Just not Miss Chambers. He pushed the *why not* question from his mind.

She shook her head. "Tell me about your trip. Did you, Smithfield, and Eastlake come up with new ways to torture Parliament?"

Not satisfied with his mother's evasive tactics, but acknowledging her wish to change the subject, he went into more detail about his meetings with the lords.

Tea arrived at the same time as Miss Chambers. She'd changed into another gown, and had fixed her hair. The smudge of dirt was also gone. Too bad, he would have liked to use his thumb to run over her soft cheek to erase it.

Merry sat across from them and poured. He leaned back and watched her graceful hands as she performed the duty. When she wasn't spewing forth outlandish opinions, she was really quite charming and sophisticated. She glanced up as she handed him a cup, and her smile warmed him for more reasons than where his thoughts normally wandered.

Miss Chambers was kind, intelligent, and from all indications, loved fiercely and protectively. She would be a stalwart wife, and a wonderful mother.

"I see you've done quite a bit already to prepare for

the Christmas season." He took the cup from Merry's hand.

"Yes. We've been very busy. I just love the holidays. All the preparations never seems like work to me." Her eyes danced with glee.

"Did you and your father entertain a lot?"

Merry nodded. "We did. He oftentimes had students over for dinner, and we would all discuss politics or some other subject of interest."

Penrose's eyes widened. "You sat in on those discussions?"

Her eyes snapped. "Of course." Then her defiant chin rose. "And why wouldn't I?"

God, he loved how quickly she went from sweet little miss to a tigress. "I don't mean to disparage you, or your father. I'm merely surprised a woman would be interested in such things."

"Oh, I suppose it would make more sense to you if I preferred to merely discuss gowns, slippers, and gossip?"

He could no longer hold back his chuckle. She narrowed her eyes, and then her lips tilted, turned into a smile, and finally she laughed.

"Ah, see, Miss Chambers. We are able to laugh at ourselves, are we not?"

"And when will it be your turn?" She smiled sweetly and took a bite of a watercress sandwich, as the dowager duchess grinned behind her cup of tea.

* * *

Merry's heart hadn't gone back to its normal rhythm since Penrose first walked into the dining room. His presence had sucked out all the air. He'd towered over her, staring down with those riveting deep brown eyes that always caused her to feel as though she'd forgotten to put on her gown.

Now with him sitting across from her, his large frame dwarfing the settee, she had a strong desire to whip out a fan to cool her heated skin. With the blood pounding in her ears, she barely heard what he and Kitty discussed. This would not do. The entire time he was gone he'd invaded her thoughts, even while she'd slept.

But, oh, how he vexed her with that superior attitude. She studied him from beneath lowered lashes. His attraction lay not just in his good looks, but the way he held himself. The way he moved across a room like a panther seeking its prey. She shivered. Would that she were his prey.

"Are you cold, Miss Chambers?" Penrose regarded her.

Cold? She was ready to rip off her clothes. "No. I'm fine."

Penrose stood. "Ladies, as much as I've enjoyed your company, there are things I must attend to before dinner." He bowed to his mother and kissed her hand, then turned to Merry. With that predatory look in his eyes, he took her hand in his, and brought it slowly to his mouth, all the time staring in her eyes. Her breath caught. He rested his lips on her hand, casting a devilish smile he did so well. "Until later."

Merry was both angry and about to self-combust. She did not want him to affect her in this manner. As he continually reminded her, he was a duke and she not even a member of the *ton*. But did he ever say that, or had she gotten that impression from Miss Jennings? She chided herself. No matter. The fact remained there could never be anything between them. And she didn't need the governess to remind her of it.

* * *

The next afternoon Merry tapped on the library door.

"Enter." The duke's deep voice rolled over her.

He sat behind his massive desk, papers scattered about, a quill pen in his hand. He glanced up as she entered, a smile gracing his lips. "Good afternoon."

"Your Grace," she curtsied.

"Merry, please stop. You keep bobbing up and down

every time you see me, and I'm becoming dizzy." He grinned. "And I'm dismayed to find we're back to 'Your Grace,' again."

She felt the blush rise to her face. "I would ask a favor, Your…"

"Yes?"

"I seek permission to allow the girls to join me outside."

"Outside? There must be a foot of snow out there." He jerked his head in the direction of the window displaying a fairyland of white glistening on tree branches.

"That's precisely why." She swallowed a giggle at his puzzled expression.

"I'm afraid I'm confused. Why would you all go out into the snow?"

"To play." She dragged out the last word.

"Play?" His puzzled expression made her laugh.

"Yes. Cavort. Have fun. Run around in the snow. Throw snowballs. Slide down the hill." She placed her hands on her hips. "Don't tell me you've never played in the snow."

He bristled. "Of course. When I was a boy."

"Ah. Maybe it's time to put all those papers aside and become a boy again."

Penrose shook his head. "Nonsense. I haven't time for that."

"In any event, may I invite the girls to go outdoors with me?"

He leaned back in his chair, eying her carefully. "That is Miss Jenning's territory. You should be asking her permission."

Merry's shoulders slumped. "I'm afraid Miss Jennings is not too receptive to my requests. Things would fare better if you gave permission. I would hate to see the girls excited and then have their hopes dashed if she says no."

He pushed back his chair and stood. "Come. We'll go to the nursery and fetch the girls. I need to stretch my legs anyway."

The sound of young voices repeating multiplication tables greeted them as they opened the school room door.

"Your Grace," Miss Jennings tittered, smoothing back her hair. Her cheeks flushed as she curtsied. "What a pleasure to have you join us." She turned to Charlotte and Clare. "Ladies, please, remember your manners. Stand and curtsy to the duke."

Both girls curtsied gracefully and wished Penrose a good day. Merry was impressed. Perhaps Miss Jennings *was* better for the girls. Merry always had too soft of a heart to discipline them.

"Miss Jennings, Miss Chambers would like to have the girls join her outside to play."

"Play?" Miss Jennings glanced at Merry, her eyes wide.

"Yes. In the snow."

Both girls jumped up and down and clapped. "Oh, please, we haven't played in the snow in ever so long," Charlotte said.

"If that is your wish, Your Grace. I don't like having their routine interrupted, but of course, I bow to your wishes." The governess's pinched face and tightened smile communicated her disapproval.

"Wonderful." He faced Merry. "They are free to join you in the snow."

"Thank you." She turned to the girls. "Come, get dressed in your warm clothes, and I'll meet you downstairs."

They quickly curtsied once again and raced from the room.

"Your Grace, if you have a moment?" Miss Jennings stopped him as he meant to leave with Merry.

"Certainly."

Merry hurried to her own chamber to put on her outdoor clothes. One of her favorite things to do was frolic in the snow. Perhaps it was a bit undignified and unladylike, but nevertheless, she indulged whenever she had the opportunity.

Still tugging on woolen gloves, she descended the stairs and greeted the girls as they hopped from one foot to the other at the front door. Even the footman's lips inched up slightly at their exuberance.

"Look what I found in the attic." Penrose walked up to them, holding two wooden sleds.

"Oh, Your Grace, thank you so much," Charlotte cried.

Each girl took a sled and disappeared through the door. Merry tightened the scarf around her neck.

"You are really going to play in the snow?" Penrose regarded her, his eyes twinkling.

"Yes I am, and if you had anything left of the child inside you, you would join us."

"Madam, I am a duke, not a school boy. I plan to stay right here where it is dry and warm."

"Coward."

He merely responded with raised eyebrows.

The sounds of the girls yelping and racing around in the snow as children had done for ages, greeted her as she stepped through the door.

Merry stood and breathed deeply of the bracing cold air. Everything always seemed magical when it snowed. Lights burning within the house, with snow decorating the roof and windowsills, soothed her with a sense of peace. The dreariness of winter would vanished and turn into a sparkling white play land.

The first order of business was building a snowman. Charlotte requested a hat, scarf, carrot, and two pieces of coal from the footman, who supplied them with a full grin on his face this time.

They all diligently rolled three different sized balls and stacked them, then decorated their effort with the supplies. The exercise warmed her, as did the lighthearted expressions on the girls' faces. Children needed to young and carefree, even when they were *ladies*.

Once the snowman stood proud in front of the manor, Charlotte and Clare spent time on the sleds, whooping with laughter when Merry took a turn and tumbled into a snow pile.

"Bravo, Miss Chambers." Penrose leaned against the front door, dressed in his greatcoat, scarf and hat. He crossed his arms and grinned as she stood and swiped snow from her pelisse.

"Have you decided to join us?" She dragged the sled toward where he stood.

"Merely to observe, I assure you."

"Sir, you need to recapture your youth. You've told me to remember my place, but it appears you need to forget your place once in a while."

"Indeed? I can assure you I never forget my place. And I find it's much wiser to enjoy watching all of you get wet and uncomfortable."

"Your Grace, we're going to make snowballs and have a snowball fight." Charlotte shouted from her position where she formed the small white balls, stacking them into a pile.

"And will Miss Chambers be joining you?"

"Of course. I always engage in the snowball fights." Merry slogged through the snow to where Clare also produced snowballs and knelt to help her. "In fact, I am the snowball queen."

"Aren't you cold, Miss Chambers?" Penrose spoke from his safe spot, a smirk on his handsome face.

Merry studied him—all stiff and proper. Dry as a bone, and watching them from his comfortable perch at the front door. A tiny niggle of awareness settled in her middle. The cold brought out the color in his cheeks, his eyes snapping with his usual arrogance. Once again she remembered the kiss in the darkness of the library. How soft and warm his mouth had been, how hard his body felt against hers.

Now he appeared lofty, above her, a reminder of how far apart they stood. Before she could even form the words for what she planned to do, she picked up a good-sized snowball, and pulling her arm back, let it fly.

The snowball whacked the duke square in the face.

"Miss Merry!" Two astonished young voices screeched.

CHAPTER EIGHT

The cold, wet mess slid slowly down Penrose's forehead, over his nose, to his tightened lips, then dripped off his chin onto his coat. He dragged his hand down his face and headed toward his nemesis.

Eyes wide, but with a huge grin, Merry rose to her feet, and turned to run. His long legs ate up the distance to her. Her skirts dragged in the snow, hampering her escape. Penrose wrapped his arm around her middle from behind. "No one has hit me in the face with a snowball in over twenty years," he growled in her ear.

Merry tugged free of his grip and promptly fell face-first into the snow when he released her. She jerked her head up, spitting out clumps of slush, still laughing. "I'm sorry." Wiping her face, she turned, and landed on her bottom. Tilting her head she regarded him. "No. I'm not sorry."

"That does it. This time, Miss Chambers, you have gone too far." Penrose wheeled and strode in the direction of the house, but made a quick detour to the pile of snowballs alongside Lady Charlotte. The young girl stared at him open-mouthed. He dropped to his knees alongside her.

"Madam, this is war," he shouted at Merry. He picked up a well-shaped ball of snow and hurled it in her direction. And hit her square on the shoulder.

"Clare, some help, please," Merry shouted in the direction where the girl stood in stunned silence.

Clare hurried to her side, and within minutes snowballs flew back and forth between the two pairs, the sound of shrieks and laughter filling the afternoon air.

* * *

Three days after the snowball fight, which Penrose took a lot of teasing about from both his mother and Brandon, the skies dumped another foot of snow.

The dowager duchess, Penrose, Merry, Lord Brandon, and Miss Jennings gathered for dinner, the dining room warm and glowing from candles and the fireplace. Footmen scurried back and forth, serving curried rabbit and pouring wine until retreating to stand quietly against the wall.

As Penrose spooned fragrant clear soup into his mouth, he regarded Merry, who looked particularly delightful tonight in a pale aquamarine silk gown. The flames from the fireplace behind her cast a shadowy mystique over her face. Then she would turn her head to comment to another diner, and the radiance of her creamy skin and full lips tempted his senses. No matter how hard he tried, she was never far from his thoughts. Nor was his desire for her.

He smiled, remembering the audacity of her dragging him into a snowball fight. It was even worth the indignity he'd put up with since that eventful incident. For the first time in more years than he could remember he hadn't felt like *the duke*. Just a man, playing in the snow with two young girls and a beautiful, mischievous woman.

That could be my family.

He shook his head. No. He liked his life just the way it was. No wife to bring complications into it. Especially one who scoffed at marriage being a business arrangement.

Let Brandon produce the necessary heir. His gut tightened. As long as his brother didn't set his sights on Merry.

"Penrose, with all this snow keeping us indoors, I'm feeling a bit restless. It's a lovely, clear evening. Perhaps you could have the sleigh brought 'round, and the horses hitched? I'm sure Miss Chambers and Miss Jennings would enjoy a ride in the night air. I know I would."

"Mother, I haven't thought of that sleigh in years. I wonder if it's still serviceable?"

"There's only one way to find out."

Penrose signaled for the footman to have the stable master locate the large sleigh and prepare it for a ride.

"I'm afraid I must decline, Your Grace. My delicate constitution doesn't allow for rides in the night air." Miss Jennings raised her chin.

"As you wish," he nodded in her direction.

"Indeed. A true lady must guard against taxing her system." She looked down her nose at Merry, then turned to smile at Penrose, and missed the way Merry glanced up at the ceiling.

He coughed to cover his laugh.

* * *

His mother and Merry stood in the entrance hall, bundled up against the cold, when Penrose jogged down the stairs. "Excellent. Are we ready?"

"My dear, I was about to mention to Miss Chambers that it appears something must not have agreed with me at dinner, and I must bow out of our little ride." His mother touched her stomach briefly and smiled sadly.

"Oh, I will stay with you." Merry immediately looked concerned.

She flicked her hand in dismissal. "Nonsense, you must both go and enjoy yourselves. I don't want to spoil the fun. Just an old lady's troubles."

"Are you sure?" Penrose regarded the rosy cheeked, very healthy looking dowager with skepticism.

"Absolutely, my dears. I will have Cook send up a

tonic. Go off and have fun. It's a lovely night for a ride." She glanced out the small window above the hall mirror. "Look at all those stars. My goodness, there must be millions of them."

"It really isn't proper for me to ride alone with His Grace," Merry said.

"Don't be silly. Who could possibility object to you both enjoying a ride on our own land? Things in the country are a bit more relaxed than in Town."

Still looking askance at the dowager, Merry allowed Penrose to take her elbow and escort her out of the house.

The shiny red sides of the conveyance gleamed in the moonlight. His heart lightened just looking at it. So many happy memories rose as he grew closer and helped Merry in. As excited as a boy, he hurried to the other side and climbed into the seat. Reaching behind him, he pulled out a large fur blanket, and tucked it securely over the two of them. "Ready?"

Merry nodded, and he picked up the reins, the jangle of the bells music to his ears. "It has been a very long time since I took a sleigh ride." He cast Merry a grin.

"It seems to me there are many things you haven't done in some time. And all of them fun."

"That's right. The duties of my title have been foremost in my life for so long, I've forgotten how to enjoy myself." He glanced at her. "But you apparently have no trouble remembering."

She shook her head and pulled the fur up to her chin. "We must always keep part of the child within us alive."

"Such philosophy. One of your father's quotes?"

Merry smiled. "No. My very own."

They flew past barren trees, ice glistening on branches that stretched upward, reaching for the multitude of stars overhead. The sound of the sleigh bells echoed in their ears, soon followed by Merry's laughter.

"This is wonderful. How could you not do this every time it snows?"

"Now with you here, you must remind me." He tugged on the reins, directing the sleigh to the left. "I want to show you something."

After about ten minutes he pulled up and brought the conveyance to a halt. The horses snorted and stomped, their warm breath visible in the cold night air. In front of them sat a frozen pond, tucked away amidst a circle of bare trees.

"My brother and I used to skate here all winter when we were youths."

"How lovely!" Merry leaned forward, taking in the ice sparkling in the moonlight. She turned to him. "We must come back here and skate."

"Oh, no thank you."

"Why ever not?" She shook her head. "Perhaps because you haven't done that either in years?" Her lips tilted in a smirk.

"You are correct, and the last thing I want to do is break my neck."

He laid his arm along the back of the sleigh and tucked an errant curl behind her ear. The moonlight on her face brought attention to her comely features. "Aren't you afraid of anything, Miss Chambers?" He lowered his voice.

She swallowed, the delicate muscles in her neck working, causing blood to race to his groin.

"Yes. There are some things I'm fearful of."

"Such as?"

Merry licked her lips, conveying images of what he'd like her to do with that sensuous mouth. He shifted and drew her closer. "I'll wager there is nothing that scares you."

"Not so, Your Grace." The words slid from her mouth on a whispered breath.

"Penrose. We dispensed with *Your Grace* a while ago." He bent toward her, leaning his forehead on hers, his hand cupping her cheek. "Do I scare you?"

She shook her head in response.

Had she discerned his thoughts at the moment, she would be petrified. Despite claiming he didn't scare her, she was certainly not unaffected by his closeness. Her pulse raced, evident by the throbbing in her neck that appeared almost painful. She drove him mad with her scent, her obvious arousal. He had to taste her, feel those soft lips under his. Gripping the back of her head, he gently rested his mouth on hers.

* * *

Penrose must've certainly heard her heart thundering in her chest. Was she afraid of him? Yes. Afraid of how he made her feel. And wish for things beyond her grasp that one only found in fairy tales.

As his warm lips covered hers, the light of a thousand candles burst behind her closed eyelids. She whimpered, and he pulled her closer. Everything inside her body throbbed. Her nipples ached where they pressed against her layers of clothing. The woman's place between her legs throbbed, then moistened. What was happening to her? She'd never felt this before, and although it frightened her, her traitorous body longed for more.

Penrose drew back and held her face gently, brushing his thumb over her heated cheek. "I want you, Merry. Very much. And *that* should scare you." Once more his head descended and he reclaimed her lips, crushing her against him. He slipped his tongue in, sweeping over the inside of her mouth, stroking, seeking all the sensitive parts. She tentatively used her tongue to meet his, spurring a groan to rumble from his chest.

He released her mouth and brushed kisses over the sensitive skin behind her ear. Shivers ran down her body.

"Are you cold?"

Quite the opposite. She wanted to remove every layer of clothing. And heaven help her, she wanted Penrose to do the same so she could rub her sensitive skin against his. Nothing in all the books and learning she'd had, prepared her for these feelings. "No, not cold. Quite the opposite, in fact. I am much overheated."

Penrose chuckled and pulled back to stare into her eyes. "You never do or say what is expected."

"'Tis a gift, Your Grace," she whispered.

"We'd better get back." He slid over and reclaimed the reins, and coldness replaced the warmth his body had provided. When she clasped her arms around herself, he pulled her to him, tucking her snugly into his side.

The ride home was swift, seeming to take much less time than their venture out. Her emotions were tumultuous, questions swimming around her mind. What would happen when they arrived home? Could they continue this back and forth dance without coming to an obvious conclusion? And what would happen afterward? Did she want to take the chance?

Penrose hopped from the sleigh and tossed the reins at the stable master. Taking Merry by her elbow, he escorted her to the house.

"I think a bit of brandy would warm us both up. Care to join me in the library, Miss Chambers?" Penrose shrugged out of his coat and peeled off his gloves. The footman helped relieve Merry of her cloak and pelisse she'd worn to keep warm. The house stood silent, a testament to its residents having retired for the night.

Although still confused by the kiss, and not sure where this would all lead, the thought of ending the night now dampened her spirits. "Yes, I think I could use a small drink."

They entered the library, and Merry rubbed her hands together and headed toward the blazing fireplace. Her heart thumped, and with the silence in the room, felt certain Penrose could hear it, and would know how he affected her. She should leave, save herself from what she wanted so badly.

"Miss Chambers." The duke's deep voice rumbled behind her as he held out a crystal glass of sherry. Her heart pounded double time as her senses came alive at his scent. She stared at his strong hand, mesmerized. What would those hands feel like against her naked flesh? She closed her eyes, but the image stayed with her.

"Thank you." She turned and cleared the squeak from her throat.

He gently touched her cheek, tenderness in his eyes.

Once they sat in front of the fire, a warm rush of memories from the other night raced through her. Only this time she wore clothes. She blushed. Why were her thoughts so wanton?

She slanted a look at Penrose, his long legs stretched in front of him. Generations of aristocracy had been bred into those features. Broad forehead, high cheekbones, and a straight nose above full lips. He studied the fire, taking unhurried swallows of brandy. Every time her gaze wandered to his mouth, a spark of awareness clenched her stomach.

He'd said he wanted her. For what? Certainly she would never suffice as his duchess. Did he intend to seduce her, and then like so many aristocrats, send her on her way, or offer her *carte blanche*? She best be on her guard where the Duke of Penrose was concerned. Perhaps Miss Jennings had been correct, and all he would seek her for would be a quick tumble.

Frustration mounted as she dwelled on how foolish she'd been already to allow his kisses. With his attractive looks, title, and money, the man before her could have any woman in England.

She dragged the remnants of her pride around her like a comforting wrap. Once Kitty's Christmas Eve ball was over, she would leave. Perhaps if Penrose decided to take a bride, it would be the governess. He seemed to hold the woman in high regard, and the girls had adjusted well to her tutelage. Although no beauty in the classic sense, Merry didn't imagine a man with Penrose's sexual appetites would find it hard to bed Miss Jennings. And produce the heir and spare.

Penrose didn't seem too interested in the usual way men of the *ton* pursued a wife. Kitty had confided that he hadn't attended *ton* activities in years. As a duke, it was his responsibility to provide the heir, not leave it to his brother, as he intended. Surely he would eventually come to that decision. And Miss Jennings agreed with his assertion that marriage was no more than a business arrangement.

Penrose drained his glass, and then set it down, pulling her from her musings. He studied her for moment, a hungry look in his eyes. Then he rose and pulled her up with both hands, wrapping his arms around her waist. "I can no longer fight this." Without further warning, he took possession of her mouth, gently at first, and then with power and persuasion. All her senses screamed, warning her to flee.

He released her lips, his warm breath causing her skin to tingle as he placed short, feathery kisses behind her ear, down her neck to her jaw. She tilted her head to give him greater access.

"Day and night, thoughts of you in my bed consume me," he murmured as he continued his assault on her senses. "I never lose control. Never." He drew back and looked in her eyes. "Until now."

Merry licked her dry lips and Penrose groaned. "I want to make love to you, breaking one of my strictest rules about bedding women under my employ."

"I am not in your employ, but your mother's," she breathed.

He cupped her chin, and brushed his thumb over her lips, his eyes darkened with desire. "What are you saying?"

Indeed. What was she saying? Was she prepared to be bedded and discarded? Could her heart take the blow? She needed to flee from this room, this man. Run as far away as she could from him and the power he held over her. Her newly formed plan to leave after Christmas must stay foremost in her mind.

Then she made the mistake of gazing into those passion-filled eyes, and inhaled deeply, opting for honesty. "I'm not sure. I've never felt this way before, and I don't know what to make of it."

He took both of her cold hands into his warm ones. "Are you aware of what I'm asking of you?"

She nodded. It was too easy to get lost in the way he looked at her. Her inner voice urged her to leave. Quickly.

His mouth took hers hungrily and she surrendered. Whatever this man wanted from her would be his. She could no longer fight it, either. The passion he elicited was more powerful than all the brandy she could consume.

He ran his hands over her back, massaging, kneading her flesh. He pulled away, and leaned his chin on the top of her head, his thumb stroking her cheek. "Tell me no now, and I will let you go. Or yes, if you wish this as much as I do." He tilted her chin up.

She hesitated only a moment. "Yes."

He swept her into his arms and strode to the door. Merry buried her face into his chest, inhaling deeply the scent that was only Penrose. Leather, brandy, and Bay Rum.

* * *

Blood pounding in his ears, Penrose sprinted up the stairs. He made short work of the distance to Merry's room. He shifted her in his arms to open the door, then closed it with a swift kick of his foot. Thank God his mother slept like the dead and wouldn't hear them.

Merry slid down his body, every delectable inch of where their bodies touched setting him on fire. He was drunk on her nearness, scent, and warmth, overwhelming him like no other woman in his life. She shuddered, reminding him he held an innocent in his arms.

He kissed her first with his eyes, then slowly with his mouth, nibbling at her lips. Her slight moan sent all his blood to the one place in his body he wanted to join with hers.

Merry slid her palms up his chest and held onto his shoulders as if anchoring herself. He prodded her lips with his tongue, and she opened, allowing him to sweep her sherry-flavored mouth. He leaned back. "I want to see you."

She drew in a breath, drawing his glance to her full breasts, the nipples prominent against her gown. Quickly his nimble fingers untied the back of the garment, drawing it down her shoulders. Two perfect orbs, their surging peaks barely hidden behind a linen chemise, dried up all the moisture in his mouth.

"You don't wear stays?"

She shook her head slightly, a slight smile gracing her lips. "No."

"What am I to do with you, Miss Chambers?" he murmured against her forehead.

She drew back and regarded him with half closed eyelids, her voice deepened with desire. "Take me to bed?"

With no idea how sensuous she sounded, she'd almost brought him to his knees. He released the grip he had on her gown and it hit the floor in a rustle of fabric. A flick of his fingers, and the straps of her chemise slid down her arms. He sucked in a breath at the creaminess of her skin, the pouting of her rose-colored nipples.

Gently he eased her onto the bed, stretching out alongside her. He fondled one generous breast, its nipple marble hard. When she arched her back in response to his touch, his tongue licked a path from her neck to nip at the rosy peak. She drew in a sharp breath as he suckled.

He shifted his head to nuzzle and kiss her other breast. "I love your response to me." He eased up on his elbow and tucked a loose tendril behind her ear. "I don't want to frighten you, sweetheart. Do you know what will happen?"

"I think so. Will it...will it hurt?"

Penrose ran his fingertips over her forehead, down her cheek to her chin. "Since you are an innocent, it will hurt a bit at first. But then I assure you, the pleasure that awaits you will more than make up for it."

"Why am I the only one with no clothes on?" The mirth in her eyes eased his concern about her fears.

"I'll correct that situation right now." He stood and tugged his shirt from his breeches.

* * *

Merry's eyes widened at the sight of the bulge in the front of Penrose's trousers. Then her gaze drifted up to his chest where he'd unbuttoned his white linen shirt and pulled it off. Her breath hitched and her stomach slid to her feet. All that golden skin, with lightly feathered dark hair down the center, leading to a place below his waist. She didn't realize she'd licked her lips until she heard his groan.

"Don't do that, or this will be over before it starts." His voice sounded strained.

Her eyelids snapped open and she stared at his flushed face. A sense of power rushed through her to know she could wring such a response from this confident, arrogant man.

He stared at her for a moment before shoving his breeches down.

Oh my God. That will never fit!

"Yes it will."

She felt the heat rise to her face, not realizing she'd spoken aloud.

Penrose climbed on the bed and ran his hand down her cheek. "Don't think so hard. Let me be concerned about how this will happen." He gathered her into his arms, once more kissing her with enough passion to turn her brain into mush and force any thoughts about size and fitting, to flee from her brain.

His strong hands skimmed up the sensitized skin of her back to grasp her shoulders, bringing their bodies together to rub her soft breasts against his hair-roughened chest. He nuzzled her neck, and she could feel his uneven breathing as he held her close to whisper into her ear. "You set me on fire, my beautiful vixen."

In a feathered touch, his fingers drifted over her ribs from under her arm to her hip, where he kneaded the globes of her bottom. No longer able to deny herself, she slid her hand to Penrose's waist, her hand wandering below until she reached that part of him that throbbed, almost as if had a life of its own.

She gasped at the feel of silk over steel. Her eyes met his as he groaned.

"Do you see what I mean? This is what you do to me."

His hand caressed the silky skin of her thigh, moving slowly up until he covered her mons. His thumb circled her most private place, and her legs fell open almost of their own accord, wanting more of the delicious feelings he evoked. He slid his finger into her body. "You're so tight."

"I told you it wouldn't fit." Would they have to stop? Maybe Penrose could think of something to make it work, for she didn't want this to end yet.

He added another finger, stretching her. "Don't worry, sweetheart."

Her body seemed to be melting down there. The sound of his fingers working her opening brought a moan from deep inside her.

"Stop thinking," he whispered before taking possession of her mouth again. Passion pounded the blood through her heart, chest and head. And where his fingers worked their magic, something began to build.

He pulled back and regarded her from under heavy-lidded eyes. Her fingers traced the beauty of his face. Scratchy along his jaw, smooth over his cheeks, and strong everywhere. When she reached his silky hair, she ran her fingers through it, urging his head back to her mouth.

"I'm sorry, love, but I need you now." He spoke against her lips.

Penrose shifted and covered her body, settling between her legs. Rising on his elbows, he brushed the damp hair from her forehead, and brought his head down in another soul-searing kiss.

She ran her hands over the sleek, smooth skin of his back. His muscles rippled under her palms as he moved. He was all hardness where she was soft. A lithe and powerful animal.

His engorged flesh prodded the area where his fingers had just been. She tensed as he edged into her channel. Surprisingly, it didn't hurt, only gave her a sense of fullness.

"I'm sorry, sweetheart, but it won't hurt for long."

Not sure what he meant, she jerked as he thrust into her body, burying himself deep inside her. Two tears leaked from the corners of her eyes at the intense sting.

"Shh, love. I hate causing you pain. Lie still for a moment and it will ease." He fingered the tears away.

As the tenderness eased, she drew in a deep breath. "It doesn't hurt anymore," she said in wonder.

Penrose withdrew his shaft almost all the way out, and then pushed back in again. He quickly set up a rhythm she picked up, meeting him thrust for thrust, flesh to flesh.

Merry moaned and licked her dry lips, unable to control her body's reaction to the wonder of their joining. Yet again the area between her legs tightened, and the sense of something wonderful awaiting her swept from her pounding heart to her very core.

He grasped her right hand with his left, keeping his weight off her with one elbow.

She tossed her heard back and forth, straining, whimpering.

"What is it, sweetheart?"

"I don't know. I feel strange, as if I need something. Something that's out there that I can't reach. Please, help me."

Penrose released her hand and reached between them

to once again fondle the part of her that brought a sigh to her lips. "Yes." Her labored breathing matched his as he worked his fingers and pounded into her.

All of a sudden Merry exploded into a thousand pieces, a downpour of fiery sensations. Her entire body throbbed as pleasure washed over her with each and every wave. Surely these feelings were not human, but mystical.

Within seconds, Penrose gave one final thrust and threw his head back with a groan, his magnificent body trembling before he collapsed over her.

They both panted as if they'd run for miles. She took in deep gulps of air and licked her dry lips. The intimate feeling of him lying on top of her as their hearts beat in rhythm lulled her into a sense of comfort and peace. She ran her fingers through his damp hair, reluctant to let him go. She savored the feeling of satisfaction, of having the weight of his body pressing hers into the mattress. Too quickly, he kissed her cheek, shifted his body, and then drew her into the pocket of his shoulder.

She closed her eyes, her breathing beginning to return to normal as a disturbing thought flitted through her mind like an epiphany.

Dear God, I'm in love with him.

CHAPTER NINE

"Miss Merry, are you even *listening* to me?" Charlotte huffed, with arms crossed, and eyes narrowed. Merry smiled. Her former charge was growing into a young lady, with all the foils and foibles of that tumultuous age. In a few short years she would make her debut and be cast upon the Marriage Mart.

"I'm sorry, dear, I was woolgathering." Merry ran her fingers down the girl's smooth cheek. "What did you say?"

"I asked if you thought His Grace would permit me to attend the Christmas Eve ball?"

"Oh, sweetheart, I don't believe so. You are much too young."

"Could you ask him? He likes you."

Merry felt the heat spread from her middle to her face. All morning she hadn't stopped thinking about last night, and *what they'd done*. After a brief kiss on her forehead, Penrose had crept from her bed in the middle of the night, leaving her bereft and hugging the pillow that still held his scent.

She had no idea how she would face him today. Would he regard her as a wanton who gave her favors freely? Nonsense. He'd been fully aware of her innocent state. She sighed. So many feelings and thoughts kept her tied in knots. As much as she wished to see him to assure herself he didn't hold her in contempt, the fear of seeing derision on his face ate at her.

Fortunately she'd been granted a reprieve since he had not appeared at breakfast. Lord Brandon informed her Penrose had left early to settle a dispute at one of his tenant's homes that had turned dangerous.

"I will ask him, darling, but don't count on it. I'm sure he will agree you are much too young for such activities."

Charlotte's face fell.

"Come, let's enjoy the freedom from your studies, and help with decorating the ballroom."

Miss Jennings had allowed both girls the afternoon off to join in the preparations for the ball and Christmas Day. Despite Merry's invitation to the governess to join them, she'd declined and murmured something about servants being available to do that type of work.

"It looks like Christmas in here." The duke's rumbling voice, along with a gust of cold air, carried from the front door, to where Merry stood in the ballroom. She immediately lost interest in directing the placement of greenery and other festive decorations.

Her stomach clenched and her heart sped up. With shaky hands, she smoothed her skirts and took a deep breath.

"So here is where you've all gathered." Penrose entered the room in a whirlwind. He kissed his mother on her cheek and glanced over at Merry, his face impassive. "Miss Chambers." He nodded.

The clenching in her stomach grew into slight nausea. Where was the warm and tender lover from last night? The man who whispered to her in the dark, who brought her to heights she'd never imagined? Sadly, the stiff and formal duke had taken his place. Then she chided herself. What did she expect him to do? Rush across the room and sweep her into his arms in front of everyone?

Yes.

"Ladies, you are doing a wonderful job. The ball tomorrow night will be a huge success thanks to all your efforts." He smiled broadly at Charlotte and Clare who tied ribbons onto greenery.

Their young faces flushed in pleasure. Did he have that effect on every female—young and old?

"My, Penrose, you are certainly in high spirits today." Kitty regarded him with amusement.

"I'm afraid I've caught your enthusiasm."

A footman entered the ballroom. "Your Grace, Miss Jennings awaits you in the library as you requested."

"Ah, yes. Miss Jennings. Thank you." He turned to the women. "I will see you all at dinner. I have several things to catch up on this afternoon." Bowing slightly, he left the room, his departure leaving her bereft.

Why would he request to see Miss Jennings?

The relief she'd hoped to feel at confronting Penrose fled. He'd treated her with the same reserve he had when she'd first arrived. Instead of the warmth from a lover, it was as if he hadn't even remembered their time together.

The beginnings of a major headache tickled the back of her neck. As soon as the work in the ballroom was finished, she'd lie down with a lavender cloth for her head.

****

Several hours later, Penrose strode into the drawing room as Brandon poured himself a brandy. He glanced at Penrose over his shoulder. "Care to join me, brother?"

"Yes. Please." Penrose walked further into the room and took the glass. "I'm glad you are the only one here. I wanted to speak with you before dinner."

His brother raised his eyebrows. "Sounds serious."

Penrose drank from his glass and motioned to the two chairs in front of the fireplace. He settled into one, and leaned forward, his elbows braced on his legs, the glass dangling from his fingers. He studied his brother. "I have decided to take a wife."

Brandon made a choking sound, then coughed and wheezed for a few minutes. Once he had himself under control, he put his glass down, and took in a deep breath. "You said you would never marry."

"I've changed my mind."

"So it seems." Brandon shifted in chair. "Miss Chambers?"

Penrose smiled. "Is it so obvious?"

"Only to everyone who has observed the two of you pretending to ignore each other."

"Ah, yes. Well, you may chide me now. To your way of thinking the giant has fallen."

"I knew it would happen one day. You never meant for me to be the heir. It was only a matter of time before you came to your senses. I am not, and never will be, fit to be the duke. I'm just surprised it has taken you this long." He raised his glass in a salute. "And may I say I congratulate you on your choice. Had you not spoken up, I would have paid my own addresses to the woman."

"Hands off, brother." Penrose narrowed his eyes.

Brandon threw up both hands, palms face out. "I would never tread on your territory."

They grinned at each other.

* * *

Merry closed the door to her bedroom and headed to the stairs. Her headache had diminished somewhat, but she'd spent the time lying in the darkened room, remembering. Perhaps it wouldn't have been so easy to do if Penrose's scent still didn't linger on the pillow where he'd slept. She had quickly changed her own sheet that the morning, horrified to see the smear of blood. The evidence of her indiscretion staring her in the face.

Her confusion at his reaction this afternoon remained. Hopefully sometime tonight they would have a few minutes alone, and she could talk to him, determine his feelings.

What feelings? You allowed him to take you to bed. You are certainly old enough to know what men think of those kinds of women.

She reached the partially open drawing room door to hear Penrose and Lord Brandon speaking. Knowing she shouldn't, nevertheless she halted and listened.

"I will announce our betrothal at the ball tomorrow night." Penrose's voice reached her ears, causing her to take in a sharp breath.

Betrothal?

"Well done for my future sister-in-law. From governess to duchess," Brandon said.

Miss Jennings? Everything inside Merry dissolved into pain. The woman had been right. With her *English* background, the duke would select Miss Jennings if he ever decided to marry. Apparently his meeting with her in the library was to propose a *business arrangement*.

Oh, how stupid she'd been. She'd given herself to a man who had no regard for her, who probably thought since she was an American, she had no morals. *Is he right?*

Merry's knees went weak. He hadn't lied. Marriage was merely a way to gain the perfect duchess, with no consideration of love. She shook her head and fought down the bile that rose to the back of her throat.

"What about the other one?"

"I have plans for her. I don't want any complications her presence would cause in my marriage. I'll see she is well taken care of and settled elsewhere."

"Won't she expect more than that? I've always felt the woman was smitten with you."

"No matter. Her false assumptions will be dealt with."

Smitten? Had the entire household noticed her attraction to the despicable man? Oh, if only the floor could open and she could drop through.

Merry stumbled backward until her heels hit the bottom stair and she fell on her bottom. She scrambled to her feet and raced up the stairs to reach her bedroom before she shattered into a million pieces.

* * *

"Obviously this will not be the typical *ton* marriage you had anticipated. Mother and I have been aware that your feelings for the girl are beyond the affection stage." He sobered and swirled the brandy in his glass. "Keep in mind, Penrose, you will hear comments from some members of the *ton* about Miss Chamber's background. Don't forget, you are considered quite the catch. I would not see her subjected to derision and heartache. I am quite fond of my future sister."

"No one will cut my duchess."

"See that they don't."

Penrose nodded as his mother and Miss Jennings entered the room.

He glanced behind them. "Where is Miss Chambers?"

"We saw her at the top of the stairs, about to return to her bedroom. Apparently she has a headache, and won't be joining us."

A line formed between his brows. "Should we send for the doctor?"

"No, dear. Miss Chambers did look a bit pale and shaky, but she assured me it was a minor thing."

The four entered the dining room, taking their seats. Despite a tempting dinner of roast duck, broiled salmon, braised beef and a selection of vegetables, Penrose remained distracted throughout the meal. Merry had seemed all right when he'd seen her this afternoon. God, how hard it had been to not race across the room and pull her into his arms, right there in front of everyone. The only way he was able to control himself was to practically ignore her.

He frowned. After dinner he would go to her room and reassure himself she wasn't seriously ill. Penrose patted his pocket to feel the sapphire and diamond ring he'd retrieved from the safe this afternoon. For generations the ring had been given to every duchess on her betrothal. It had been hard not to confide in his mother, but as much as he loved the woman, she would likely spoil the surprise before he had the chance to propose to Merry tomorrow evening, right before the ball.

Penrose smiled to himself. He'd had no idea when his annoyance with Merry had changed to desire, and then to something akin to love. Hell, it *was* love. He loved the minx, and without a doubt her escapades would bring a certain amount of terror to his well-ordered life. He couldn't wait.

Although he tried unsuccessfully to pay attention to the conversation around him, he was blessedly relieved when the meal came to an end.

"I will see you all in the morning. I have matters to attend to this evening. Good night." Penrose pushed his chair back and left the room.

He hurried up the stairs, then strode down the corridor to Merry's room, and tapped on the door.

"Yes." Her voice sounded muffled, like she had a stuffed nose. Was she very sick?

"Merry, open the door."

"I'm sorry, Your Grace, but I'm not feeling well."

Your Grace?

"That is precisely why I want you to open the door. Should I send for the doctor?"

"No!"

He rattled the latch. "Merry, can you please let me in? I won't stay, I just want to assure myself of your condition."

"I have no *condition*, Your Grace."

He ran his fingers through his hair in frustration. What was going on? Had their lovemaking last night upset her? He had an almost frantic need to see her, run his hands up and down her body, make sure she was all right.

"Merry, I'm asking nicely. Now please open the door."

"I'm not properly dressed, Your Grace."

He leaned his forehead on the door. Something was drastically wrong, and unless he could actually view her, he knew sleep would not come to him tonight. A sense of dread descended on him.

"All right. Shall I have a tray sent up?"

No answer.

"Merry?"

Her sigh came through the door. "No. Please leave me."

"Miss Chambers, I am not leaving here until you open the door. If necessary, I will have a footman remove it for me."

After a very long minute, the lock snapped and the door opened only far enough for him to see her puffy face in the shadows.

His gut clenched. "You look as if you could use a doctor."

She shook her head. "I'm fine."

"Can I come in and speak with you for a minute?" She was obviously very upset, and the only thing he could think of was last night. He needed to hold her, assure her all was well, and he—God help him—had fallen in love with her.

"No. I need to sleep. As you can see, I am fine. I do not need a doctor. Good night." She closed the door, turned the lock, and he soon heard the sound of a heavy piece of furniture being dragged in front of the door.

Stunned into silence, he headed to his room.

* * *

Gasping from the effort of shoving the heavy table in front of the door, Merry slid down the wall and hugged herself, the sound of Penrose's receding footsteps a wound to her heart. Why had he come? A man about to offer a betrothal to one woman, should not seek to enter the room of another.

Unless he expected to continue what they'd done last

night? She sat up, her jaw slack. Did he intend to marry Miss Jennings, and have Merry for a mistress? Of course. Thus his comment about *having plans for her* and *seeing her settled elsewhere*.

All the agony of the past hour segued into anger. How dare the man! He intended to set her up in another house where he could visit her whenever he chose. He was by far the most vile, arrogant, miserable excuse for a human being she'd ever met. He would marry one woman, then break his marriage vows with another. Well, he would certainly get a piece of her mind the next time she saw him.

She embraced the anger that kept her misery at bay. When the man made his indecent proposal to her, she would box his ears back and walk away with her head held high and her pride intact.

Unlike my innocence, which is long gone.

CHAPTER TEN

The next morning, Penrose entered the breakfast room and scowled. "Where is Miss Chambers?"

His mother looked up from her place at the table, nibbling a piece of toast. "Here and gone."

"What do you mean?"

"She was finishing up her breakfast when I arrived. I had several things for her to do in town this morning, so she set out early."

He took in a large breath and pulled out a chair. "How long will she be gone?"

"My, you're full of questions this morning." She shot him a curious look.

Penrose shrugged. No point in making his mother suspicious. "No matter. I only wondered how she felt this morning, considering her illness last evening."

His mother frowned. "Actually, she was rather quiet and pale, but she said her head felt better."

A sense of relief filled him, but given Merry's strange behavior when he went to her room last night, he wouldn't feel completely relaxed until he saw her. Still confused by her actions and her obvious distraught state, all he wanted to do was gather her close and take away all her fear. For it must certainly had been fear that plagued her. As an innocent, she must surely have conflicting feelings about their lovemaking.

Hopefully she wouldn't take it into her mind that he would make love to her and not propose marriage. Perhaps she was under the impression he would ask for her hand only because he'd taken her innocence. His gut tightened in frustration. He needed to talk to her. Now.

"Good morning, Your Grace." Miss Jennings swept into the room, her head held high as if she were the duchess. She nodded in his mother's direction. "Good morning to you as well, Your Grace."

Penrose stood, then held out a chair for her. She blushed and settled herself. "I'm so looking forward to tonight's festivities." She batted her eyelashes at him.

Good Lord. His brother had been correct. It appeared Miss Jennings was smitten with him. More likely his money and title. He recalled the meeting with her yesterday afternoon to assess his wards' progress in their studies. At the time, his thoughts were so consumed with Merry, he never paid attention to the governess's actions.

Considering the disdain she held for his future duchess, things would definitely run smoother if he helped her secure another position. As soon as Merry accepted his offer, he would begin searching among his acquaintances for a suitable place for Miss Jennings.

But now his attention totally focused on his soon-to-be betrothed. The passion in her, just waiting to be unleashed, brought the blood racing to his groin. A small taste of her the other night had left him craving more. Their engagement would have to be very short, lest the future Duke of Penrose make an appearance too soon after their wedding vows. He chuckled.

Never had he envisioned a woman would so possess him that he would change his mind not only about marrying, but throwing the *business arrangement* part of it out the window.

"Your Grace?" Miss Jennings questioned him.

Pulling himself back to his surroundings, he glanced at her. "Yes?"

"I said, do you imagine this will be the first of many balls at Penrose Hall?"

He stared at her, running her words through his brain, still trying to figure out what she asked him. And where the devil was Merry? Why wasn't she the one sitting here next to him, smiling, and asking about future balls? He shook his head, years of training taking over. "I'm sure my mother will enjoy planning many more festivities in the future."

Penrose placed his serviette alongside his plate and stood. "Now if you will excuse me, ladies, I will retire to my library to finish up some last minute items before our overnight guests arrive."

Despite his pronouncement, when he entered the library, he headed to the window, his hands clasped behind his back. He gazed out at the dreary day. Snow was once again in the air.

* * *

Merry checked the yellow and white flowered china clock on her dresser. Her lady's maid would arrive shortly to help her into her gown and fix her hair. She placed her hands over her middle to stop the fluttering.

She'd managed to avoid Penrose all day. When she arrived home from the small market town, he'd been behind closed doors with his steward. Breathing a sigh of relief, she scurried to her room, where she remained hidden for the afternoon.

Now with her bath over, and coming to terms with her impending meeting with Penrose, all the jumbled thoughts that had raced through her mind all day began to form cohesive sentences. She would let him make his scandalous proposal. But to make certain he knew she understood what he planned to do, she'd selected her most indecent gown. If he believed her to be a woman of loose morals, then she would play the part.

The low cut white silk garment, with a wide band of red satin underneath her breasts brought attention to the creamy skin of her cleavage. The small cap sleeves emphasized her slender shoulders. As she gazed at the beautiful gown, she tapped her finger against her lips. Perhaps she would even dampen the material so it clung to her body. She shivered, reminding herself it was December.

She padded across the room to her chest and withdrew long red satin opera gloves. Perfect to finish off the outfit that declared her to be a woman of little virtue, as he apparently saw her. She would tempt the man all evening, teasing him with what he would never again have. Then when he offered to make her his mistress, she would slap his arrogant face, then storm away, her head held high.

Why didn't that make her feel any better? True, she would have her moment, but she'd have to leave her girls and Kitty. And watch Miss Jennings preen.

But worse than anything, she'd lose the man she loved. The man she'd given herself to and thought he had at least some feelings for her besides lust. *To us marriage is all a business arrangement, nothing more.*

Oh God, how am I going to get through this night?

* * *

Penrose adjusted his cravat once more, standing next to his mother in the receiving line, constantly watching the staircase, waiting for Merry to descend. His heart sped up every time he caught a flash of blonde out of the corner of his eye. When the woman turned out not to be Merry, his heart resumed its normal pattern.

Where was the woman?

For some inexplicable reason, he'd been unsuccessful in seeing her all day. Every time he asked for her, she was gone from the manor, locked in her room, busy with his wards, supervising the servants, or on some infernal mission for his mother. If he didn't know better, he'd swear Merry had purposely avoided him.

Unlike the other women, she elected to have a tray sent to her room for dinner. His stomach in knots, he ate very little, and drank too much. He grunted. Leave it to getting involved with a woman to drive a man to drink.

"You're looking quite well, Your Grace." His musings were interrupted by Lady St. James, as she eyed him, the familiar sultry look in her eyes. He'd had a short dalliance with her a few years ago, but quickly lost interest. Now her blatant tone and the possessive way she rested her hand on his chest rankled.

"My lady," he bent over her hand and kissed it.

She cast a glance at him from under shuttered eyelids, a siren's smile on her face before she moved along.

"Your Grace." He turned to encounter Miss Jennings standing beside him. Heavens, what did the woman have on? Her gown would be more appropriate for a young debutante. Did she not possess anything more suited to her age? Ever the gentleman, he bent and kissed her hand. "You're looking lovely this evening."

She tittered, and lingered, fussing with her gown. The overpowering stench of her perfume caused his eyes to water. He glanced up and came eye to eye with Merry making her way into the ballroom.

Everyone else in the room ceased to exist. He attempted to swallow with the driest mouth he'd ever had. His eyes ate her up, her cool assessment, her chin angled in arrogance. Her tongue ran over her lush lips as her gaze swung back and forth between him and Miss Jennings. She was exquisite.

And barely dressed! God's teeth! Where the devil was the rest of her gown?

His blood froze, unable to decide whether to race downward to his groin in lust, or upward to his head in anger. If she took a deep breath and exhaled, her delectable breasts would tumble from her bodice into her drink. All the muscles in his gut tightened, and he fought a powerful desire to shrug out of his jacket, then whip it around her shoulders, covering up what no one else except he should ever lay eyes on.

He snagged her hand as she passed by.

She stopped, and raised her chin. "Your Grace," she curtsied gracefully.

"Stand up," he snapped, causing his mother to glance at him. He could swear he'd gotten a glimpse of her nipples. "Do not curtsy for the rest of the evening."

"As you say." Merry rose, a sly smile on her face.

Her eyes twinkled with mirth, the cool disdain on her features a marked contrast. His grip tightened on her hand. The red satin glove on her warm fingers brought a flush to his face, sending his blood south. "Don't go anywhere. I want to speak with you."

"Indeed, Your Grace?" She tugged her hand from his. "If you will excuse me, I believe I'm being summoned." She nodded slightly and entered the ballroom.

Good lord, I can't let her parade around the room in that gown!

Twenty very long minutes passed before the last guest had been greeted, and Penrose was free to find his future duchess. After searching through the throng, he finally spotted her talking with Lord Grey, one of London's worst rakes. He headed in her direction, his blood pumping in rhythm with his steps.

* * *

She should never have worn this gown. If one more *gentleman* talked to her breasts, she would scream. The gentleman introduced to her as Lord Grey had cornered her a while ago, and kept moving closer than what was acceptable. If only she could loosen one of her hairpins to stick his hand.

Once more she edged away from him and turned her head to see Penrose striding toward them, his face a mask of fury. She stiffened her spine, ready to do battle.

Her stomach released a horde of butterflies. Why did he have to look so good? A myriad of eyes watched him from above silk fans as he strode past. Her heart hammered at the sight of his broad shoulders as he eased his way through the crowd. Dark waves of silky hair fell over his forehead, drawing her attention to his eyebrows, furrowed above piercing brown eyes. She gulped. This would be much easier to do if she didn't have to look at him.

He gripped Grey's shoulder. "Grey. I believe Lady St. James is looking for you."

About to object, Lord Grey backed away when he observed Penrose's face. "Thank you, Your Grace."

Penrose took her gloved hand in his, kissed it, then staring into her eyes, swept her into the first dance. All the arrogance of His Grace, Duke of Penrose, emanated from his hard body.

Heat diffused her face at the memory of that arrogance cracking under the spell of their shared passion. Her flesh tingled where his palm gripped her back. As he brought them into a turn, he pulled her closer. His dancing was as graceful as everything else about him.

"It appears I will have to replace your lady's maid." His deep voice swept over her like a curtain of fire.

Unable to speak, Merry didn't reply, but merely raised her eyebrows.

His jaw worked. "She seems to have forgotten the rest of your gown."

Merry lifted her chin. All the cutting remarks she'd worked out in her mind throughout the day had fled at Penrose's touch. Why did he affect her so? Where was the anger she'd felt last night after hearing his intention to become betrothed to Miss Jennings?

After making love to me.

Gathering the mantle of righteous indignation about her, she cast him a tight smile. "This gown is precisely the way it should be. And you have no right to criticize my choice of clothing."

"And that will soon change." He moved them toward the French doors, and then grasping her hand tightly, all but dragged her onto the terrace.

"Your Grace, it's freezing out here." She ran her palms up and down her arms.

"We need a quiet place to talk, and I don't want to march you through that room with every man in there staring at your bosom." He shrugged out of his jacket and wrapped it around her.

She pulled the jacket closer. "'Tis *my* bosom to stare at." The warmth from his body transferred itself to her, along with his scent, crippling her heart.

"Merry." He took both her hands in his. "I've been trying see you alone all day."

"Under the circumstances, Your Grace, 'tis very inappropriate."

He slid his arms around her, then gathered her close. "But not for long. What I'm about to ask you will make it acceptable for me to be alone with you any time I wish."

The blood rushed to her face. The nerve of the man. Not only was he going to expect her to be his mistress, he would also demand her time and attention any time he chose. Oh, how her palm itched to smack that smug face.

"Indeed?" She raised her eyebrows, all the time dying on the inside.

He cupped her chin. "Miss Chambers, I am requesting you do me the honor of becoming my duchess."

Her heart pounded in righteous indignation. She reared back. "How dare you? You think because…" She stopped and stared at him wide-eyed. "What?"

"I'm asking you to marry me, sweetheart."

Merry stared at him in shocked silence, then shook her head. "Marry you?"

"Yes."

"What about Miss Jennings?"

"Who?"

"Miss Jennings. The perfect governess who would be the perfect duchess."

"What are you talking about?" He cupped her cheek. "You, my love, are the perfect duchess. For me."

When what he'd said finally sunk in, Merry realized she'd misunderstood the entire conversation she'd overheard between Penrose and Lord Brandon.

"You wish to marry *me*?" she whispered.

"More than anything." He brushed his lips over hers. "Sweetheart, please save me from the torture I've been going through all day and say yes."

She moved back, hand on her hip, her eyes narrowed. "Is this to be a *business arrangement*, Your Grace?" She tapped her foot.

He grinned and tugged her back. "No, my love." He tapped the end of her nose with his finger. "And no more 'Your Grace.' I want to be your husband, your lover, the father of your children. And if you feel about me the way I feel about you, this will be a love match."

Tears of relief and joy gathered in her eyes. This man, who she'd fallen so deeply in love with, would be hers. No matter to him that he was the duke, and she a mere American, he loved her. Her chest swelled with happiness. "Oh yes, this will definitely be a love match."

"Miss Merry!" Charlotte and Clare called from one of the upper windows.

Both Merry and Penrose sprang apart and look upwards. Merry gasped. "Girls, what are you doing hanging out the window in your night clothes?"

"It's midnight, Miss Merry. Christmas Day." They grinned at her, their beautiful young faces aglow in the moonlight.

She tried unsuccessfully to hide her smile. "Return to your room, I will deal with you in the morning."

Penrose threw back his head and laughed.

Merry attempted to glare at him, but lost the battle. "Don't laugh. They are in big trouble."

As the first snowflakes fell, he gathered her close yet again, then leaned his forehead on hers. "Merry Christmas, Miss Merry."

"Look, His Grace is kissing Miss Merry," Charlotte sighed. "Isn't it wonderful?"

EPILOGUE

One Year Later

"Your Grace, what are you doing out of bed?" The young servant hurried to Merry's side, gripping her elbow as if she were an invalid.

"I am finished with lying about in bed. My son is two weeks old, and I refuse to spend another day staring at the ceiling."

"I don't know, I'm afraid His Grace will be furious."

"Indeed he will be." Penrose strode down the corridor, scooped Merry up into his arms, and started up the stairs.

"For heaven's sake, put me down. I can walk."

"No. The accoucheur distinctly said you were to remain in bed for three weeks."

"I would love to see how you would behave if someone told you to stay in bed for three weeks."

"I did not just deliver a baby, madam."

"But I feel fine. I need some exercise. I can help with the preparations for Christmas."

"No. I will settle you in bed, and have tea sent up. You must re-gain your strength so you can properly care for my son."

She glared at him. "My son, too."

"My goodness, what is all the bickering about?" The dowager duchess stood at the end of the corridor, her hands planted on her hips.

"Penrose insists I must return to bed."

"Where she will remain for another week."

With a shake of her head, the dowager opened the door to the duke's apartments and Penrose marched through, and headed directly to the large canopied bed in the middle of the room. He deposited his wife onto the mattress and pulled up the covers. "Stay here."

* * *

To Penrose's dismay, Merry covered her face with her hands and burst into tears.

"Oh, my dear," the dowager soothed as she hurried forth and sat next to Merry on the bed. "It is difficult, I know." She glared at her son.

He stretched out his palms in supplication. "What did I say?"

"Miss Merry, guess what? Lord Brandon said we can all go ice skating this afternoon." Lady Charlotte entered the room, buttoning her pelisse.

Merry rolled over and cried harder.

"What's the matter with Miss Merry?" Clare followed Charlotte's footsteps.

They all stood staring at the woman sobbing on the bed. The dowager cupped her jaw in her palm and shook her head. The girls clutched each other's hands.

"Everyone out!" Penrose's decree had the dowager and girls scurrying to the door.

Once the door closed, he stood, his hands clasping open and closed as he walked slowly to the bed. "Sweetheart?"

She didn't answer, just took a shuddering breath.

Sighing, he sat next to her and pulled her into his arms. "I am so sorry, my love."

She hiccupped and curled into his chest, almost as if she could crawl under his skin. "I don't know why I'm crying." She took the handkerchief he handed her and blew her nose. "I have a beautiful, healthy baby, and I feel fine. There is nothing to be unhappy about. Is there?"

He smoothed the hair back from her forehead. "Mother tells me all women have these 'spells' after childbirth. It will pass."

"If only I could feel useful. Nanny brings the baby to me a few times a day, but then whisks him right back after I feed him. She says he needs to be bundled in his bed all the time." She looked at him, tears clumping her eyelashes. "I want to hold him, play with him, count his fingers and toes. Maybe sing him a lullaby."

Gently, he rubbed the back of her neck until he felt her tightened muscles relax. Apparently the way Polite Society dealt with its children by handing them off to a nanny, then a governess, was not going to work for his wife. Thinking back, it rarely worked for his mother, as well.

"All right, let's go." Once more he settled her into his arms and strode to the door.

"Where are we going?"

"To make you useful."

"Bess, fetch Her Grace's bedding and bring it down to the drawing room." He barked his orders at the young maid which had her scurrying to do his bid.

Once they reached the drawing room, Penrose deposited Merry in a chair next to the fireplace. She inhaled deeply of the pine scented room, smiling warmly at the tree the footmen had brought into the house yesterday. The girls had been busy making decorations and placing them on the branches.

With his wife in confinement, there would be no Christmas Eve Ball this year, but he needed to work harder to make this a pleasant Christmas for her.

"Make up the settee so Her Grace can recline there."

He motioned to Bess as she entered the room, with a footman following holding sheets, blankets and a pillow.

Once the bed was made up, and assured that Merry was comfortable, Penrose left the room. "Don't go anywhere, I will be right back."

* * *

Merry grinned as Penrose kissed her on the forehead and strode from the room. How her opinion of him had changed since the day she had arrived with the girls in tow. At that meeting she would never have guessed what a caring, tender husband he would be. Of course, he was still arrogant and overbearing at times, but he more than made up for it in the way he tried so hard to please her.

"Well this is certainly a nice compromise." Kitty placed a bowl of pine cones on the table near the door and surveyed the area. "This is a much more pleasant place for you to recuperate."

"I don't need to recuperate. I feel fine."

"Yes, I know dear, and when I had my sons I felt fine as well, but to keep my husband happy I stayed in bed for weeks. Longer than three, it seems to me." She tapped her lips with her index finger. "Or maybe it just seemed so much longer."

"Miss Merry we decided to stay with you instead of skating." Lady Clare skipped into the room.

Lord Brandon followed. "Can I tell you, dear sister, how happy I am to be forced to stay in the nice warm house instead of freezing my—"

"Brandon!" the duchess warned.

"Sorry, Mother. But I wouldn't have said what you think." He winked and took the seat across from Merry. "Feeling lonely, were you?"

"A bit," she sighed.

"Perhaps we can have a game of charades later. Watching Penrose make a fool of himself will certainly entertain you."

"Well, look who we have here." Penrose strolled

through the doorway with a small bundle wrapped in a soft white blanket. "I found this tyke lying around up in the nursery. Thought I would put him to good use."

Merry held her arms out, her fingers flexing to hold her child.

Penrose placed the baby gently in her arms. "Here you are, Your Grace. Just as you requested. William Thomas, the Marquis of Burlington." Penrose settled alongside his family. His large finger traced the softness of the newborn's skin. "Merry Christmas, my son."

"This is such a wonderful Christmas," Merry choked. Then the tears fell as she hugged her baby close.

The End

Did you like this story? Please consider leaving a review on either Goodreads or the place where you bought it. Long or short, your review will help other readers discover new authors and make purchasing decisions!

Please turn the page for an excerpt from *Seducing the Marquess*.

Richard, Marquess of Devon, and his wife, Eugenia, have been married five months. They have the perfect ton marriage. Respect and affection, with no messy entanglement such as love. Soon after Devon's mistress dies, Eugenia stumbles onto a naughty book in a bookstore. A book that explains all the things proper ladies of the ton are unaware of, and would never consent to do with their husbands.

Once Eugenia acquires the book—scandalously—she begins a campaign to make sure her husband has no reason to replace his mistress.

Although Devon has continued to visit his paramour since his marriage, all they've done is play cards. Devon's rigid upbringing impressed upon him that gentlemen slake their baser needs on a mistress, not their gently bred wives. However, once married, he was no longer comfortable bedding a woman other than Eugenia.

As bored matrons and eager widows toss him veiled invitations while he wrestles with this dilemma, his wife has begun to change. No longer the prim and proper woman he courted and married, her behavior leads him to an alarming conclusion. . .

SEDUCING THE MARQUESS

Chapter One

"A woman who seeks a man's attentions will do the unexpected."

Secrets of the Bedchamber, p. 27

October, 1819
London, England

Lady Eugenia Devon's ears perked up when she heard the name *Mrs. Forestor* whispered by Lady Marlboro to Lady Stevenson. Unobtrusively attempting to overhear their conversation, she sipped her tea and endeavored to block out the constant blathering by Mrs. Fairchild, who had held her ears captive for more than twenty minutes.

Ever so slightly, she tilted her head in the direction of the women. "Yes, my dear, it appears she died yesterday morning. Her carriage overturned on the road from Bath. Poor thing broke her neck." Lady Marlboro looked around and continued on, her effort to whisper falling somewhat flat. "It was quite a shock, a woman so beautiful." They both glanced in Eugenia's direction, the smirks on their faces cutting her heart.

So my husband's mistress is dead.

If she felt anything at all it was more like numbness. How many times had she wished the woman out of her life? Not that she had wished her ill, but she hardly felt remorse.

She remained still, with her much-practiced smile on her face, never missing a sip of her tea. Anyone observing her would surely think she hadn't heard the whispers, and if she had, they had no effect on her. Her fingers did not shake as she placed her teacup in the saucer. Her hands lay in her lap; she did not fidget or glance at the women who were gossiping. She did not rise and excuse herself to her hostess and hurry from the room.

As always, The Ice Queen was in complete control of herself.

A half hour later, when she deemed enough time had passed, she rose and called for her carriage. She thanked Mrs. Fairchild and offered a genuine smile to Ladies Marlboro and Stevenson. As she left the room, head held high, she did not even hesitate when she heard, "She's such a cold woman. No wonder Devon kept his mistress."

Her smiled remained in place as her carriage rode through the streets of Mayfair. Once they arrived at her townhouse, she accepted the footman's hand and made her way up the steps to the front door. She turned so her butler, Bellows, could remove her pelisse. Gracefully, she climbed the stairs to her bedchamber, floating along, as was her usual gait.

She entered the familiar room, decorated in pale rose and green. The room was perfect, much as she was. Not one hairpin out of place, either in her room or on her person. She laid her reticule on the dressing table and bent to remove her half boots.

Then she threw herself on her bed, her hands over her head, grinning foolishly at the canopy. Waves of joy washed over her, and she had the urge to jump up, race to the window, and fling it open, shouting like a fishwife for all of London to hear.

Her nemesis was dead!

***

The Marquess of Devon heard of the death of his former mistress while sitting in his club, sipping brandy. When the young pup who was having a good time spreading the news blurted it out to him, Devon's hands fisted on his glass. His heart took a quick thump and then he was surprised at the sense of relief that flooded him, followed by shame at not feeling more than that.

He nodded at offered condolences as he left the club and headed for home. Not that the townhouse in Mayfair was more of a refuge than one of his clubs. His townhouse was the place where he kept his clothing and worked at his desk in the library. Where he made the requisite three trips a week from his bedchamber to his wife's for the purpose of getting her with child.

But he had no desire to put up with the shrewd glances and speculations that were surely to come if he remained at White's.

He entered the mews, turned his horse over to the stable master, and took the stairs up to his house. He wondered if Eugenia had heard the news. As a polished and proper member of the *ton*, his wife would not acknowledge Margaret's death. Neither would he. They'd never spoken of his former mistress, indeed as far as everyone was concerned, including Eugenia, he had still visited her for sex.

As he approached his bedchamber, he didn't realize the lateness of the hour until the bell sounded to dress for dinner.

His valet, Jake, awaited him. "Good evening, my lord. I have your bath ready."

"Thank you, and this evening her ladyship and I will be attending the Ponsoby ball."

"Yes. I have the proper attire for the event ready," the man sniffed. Too well-trained to show he needn't a reminder, since Jake knew Devon's schedule better then he himself did, nevertheless Devon sensed the slight rebuke.

Two hours later, Devon held up the crystal decanter as Eugenia settled on the blue and white striped chair in the drawing room, where they awaited the dinner announcement. "Would you care for a sherry, my dear?"

"Yes. Thank you, my lord."

Always formal, his wife was the epitome of what he'd wanted when he'd begun his search for a marchioness. Tonight she wore a gown of pale blue shot through with silver. Her golden blond hair was pulled back into a chignon at her nape. No dangling curls brought softness to her features as she regarded him with ice blue eyes.

He handed her the glass and sat across from her, sipping a brandy. "Are you looking forward to the ball tonight?"

A slight hesitation caught his notice. Odd. Eugenia never hesitated. "Yes, indeed I am."

Had she already heard of Margaret's death and was concerned about gossip? No. His wife never noticed, nor participated in, gossip.

The door to the drawing room opened, and Bellows entered, stiff as was his usual demeanor. Bowing slightly, he said, "I apologize for the interruption, my lady."

Eugenia smiled up at him, despite the fact that Devon had never seen his butler smile back. "Yes, Bellows, what is it?"

"The upstairs maid, Jennie, has requested an audience. I told her to speak with the housekeeper, but she insisted on speaking with you. She indicated she would wait all evening if necessary." The butler appeared as though he smelled something unpleasant on the bottom of his shoe.

"You may send her in." Eugenia placed her glass on the table.

Not wishing to deal with servant issues—after all, wasn't that one of the reasons he'd wanted a wife?— Devon stood, "I will leave you to deal with this."

"No," Eugenia held out her hand. "Please stay, my lord. If you are uncomfortable, you can pick up a book and pretend to read. I am sure this won't take long, and then we can move on to dinner."

He acquiesced and headed to the sideboard to refill his brandy glass. He still would have preferred to remove himself, but since she requested he remain, he would bear it.

Devon recognized the chit when she entered. A slight girl, and whether she was attractive or not was unknown since her face was swollen with tears. She crushed a handkerchief between her fingers and moved to stand in front of Eugenia.

It seemed to him she'd been employed for some time now. Certainly before he and Eugenia had married. Another reason he was grateful for his wife. He detested dealing with servant issues.

"Yes, Jennie. Bellows said you wished to speak with me."

She curtsied. "Oh, my lady, I am so sorry for interrupting you. I feel so bad, but something has come up that I..." The girl burst into tears, blubbering into her soaked handkerchief.

Devon glanced at Eugenia, who looked back at him, her eyebrows raised.

"Perchance you might tell me what your problem is?" Eugenia's soft voice encouraged the girl to pull herself together.

Sniffing, she said, "I believe I am with child, my lady."

"Indeed." Something in that one word must have encouraged the maid, because she seemed to draw strength from it.

"Is she married?" Devon mouthed to Eugenia, who

gave a curt shake of her head.

He sipped his brandy, feeling sorry for Jennie, about to lose her position with a child on the way.

"Who is the father, Jennie?" Eugenia continued in a voice that appeared to calm the maid.

"Mick," she mumbled, casting a glance at Devon.

Devon nearly choked on his brandy. "My groom?"

"Yes, my lord." This was the first time the girl had directly looked at him since she'd entered the room. He was getting more and more uncomfortable with the conversation. Why the devil had he been dragged into this? These matters should not be brought up while he was around. Most likely, Eugenia would dismiss them both.

If he'd been surprised by the entire exchange, he was completely taken aback when Eugenia turned to him and said, "You must insist your groom marry Jennie immediately."

"What?"

Eugenia lifted her chin. "Jennie is a good girl. If she is in a family way, she is not the only one responsible." She turned to the maid, who regarded his wife with something akin to adoration. "You may go about your duties. His lordship will take the matter in hand."

"Oh, thank you, my lady." Jennie burst into tears once again and fled the room, the twisted handkerchief sopping the waterfall.

Eugenia regarded him, determination in her blue eyes. "I will leave the situation in your capable hands, my lord."

She retrieved her glass of sherry and took a sip. "Has there been progress on the bill you are sponsoring in Parliament?"

He was afraid he appeared dimwitted as he stared at her slack-jawed. She had just handled a most distressing situation with grace and aplomb. Now she wanted to continue on as if something extraordinary had not just occurred.

He mentally shook himself and collected his

thoughts. "Yes, I have managed to gather a bit more support for it."

Of course, he mused, there was much more to the gathering of support, but since women were unable to grasp politics, there was no reason to expound on that. Truth be known, he'd always questioned such an assumption drilled into him by his father. He and Eugenia had had several conversations where she'd surprised him with her intelligence and insight.

Although, after the scene he'd just witnessed, he was hard-pressed to admit he really knew his wife at all. He saw Eugenia as a compassionate person, but her handling of the maid's situation impressed him. Surely, had his own mother, or any other woman of the *ton* he'd known, been faced with a similar situation, they would have dismissed both servants with no recommend.

And they called *her* The Ice Queen.

They fell silent, the only sound the ticking of the longcase clock in the corner of the room. He refused to move onto the subject of the weather. Why was it he had never noticed until now how little they had to say to each other? Mayhap if he'd encouraged her thoughts on the bill he was sponsoring, he would once again see her enthusiasm as she voiced her opinion. Keeping to certain subjects when conversing with one's wife made for stilted discussions.

His thoughts wandered as he sipped his brandy and Eugenia stared into the fire, a picture of female serenity. He'd wanted a wife he could count on to always do the right thing, handle every issue that came up in his household without troubling him, who was both beautiful and gracious. No hint of scandal had ever been, nor ever would be, associated with her name. When he'd decided the time was right to set up his nursery, he had not wavered from his choice. He had wanted The Ice Queen and had gone after her with the same determination as he did all things.

He had paid her the necessary court once he'd received the approval of her brother. After an acceptable period of time, he'd met with Lord Clarendon again and had worked out the marriage contracts, then he'd proposed to Eugenia, anticipating her acquiescence. She had accepted with grace and charm and had presented her cool hand for his kiss. They'd had a lavish wedding under the eyes and good wishes of the *ton*.

Everything had been perfect from then on, so why was he now experiencing this sense of restlessness, of wishing they had more to say to each other?

Wanting to break the silence, he said, "I was quite impressed with your handling of the servant issue just now, Eugenia."

She actually looked surprised at his remarks. "Thank you, my lord. I am sorry you had to be a witness to the matter, but I already had a hint of the situation and hadn't wanted to discourage the poor girl by having you leave the room as though she'd done something wrong in requesting my attendance."

He sipped his drink. "You knew of her condition?"

"I didn't know, but suspected. 'Tis not hard to know the concerns and happenings of the staff when one keeps an eye and ear open."

Another reason to be grateful for his choice in a spouse. Matters of staff and household concerns, and their resultant problems, rattled him. Before Eugenia, he'd left it all up to his housekeeper, who in turn ended up consulting with him, anyway. "Yes, I can see where that would be true. Well, I wish to thank you for your management of what could have been a very unpleasant circumstance."

She dipped her head in acknowledgment of his words, a slight blush rising to her lovely cheeks.

He was beginning to realize that Eugenia was so much more than merely a proper lady. Underneath her shell of decorum, he sensed a warm, loving woman, anxious to throw off the mantle of aloofness that no doubt had been impressed upon her by tutors and governesses. To his amazement, that realization was leading him to question other parts of marriage directed by his father.

As a member of the nobility, it was his obligation to fill his nursery. He visited Eugenia's bed on a regular basis. Other than those obligatory appearances to ensure succession, he reminded himself one was not expected to feel lust or love for one's wife. To do so was considered crass and bad *ton*.

It annoyed him that the butler's announcement of dinner brought a certain amount of relief. Life was perfect, he assured himself, and exactly as he had planned. He didn't need uncomfortable thoughts that made him question things better left alone.

At precisely ten o'clock they left the house. Arm in arm they proceeded down the stairs into the waiting carriage. As they rode through Mayfair, Eugenia seemed to grow tense. Perhaps she was, indeed, expecting some unpleasantness tonight due to Margaret's death.

Only he and Margaret had known they had not been in bed together since the night before his wedding. Despite his belief that a proper gentleman maintained a mistress in order not to upset his wife's delicate sensibilities, he had not been able to bring himself to continue their relationship. In fact, the entire situation had become ridiculous.

The last time he'd visited her they'd played cards until the wee hours of the morning. More than once she had indicated she would not be averse to putting out that she was looking for a new protector. However, Devon had been reluctant to do so, and could never understand why.

Once they arrived at the ball and greeted their host and hostess, he and Eugenia danced their one set together, this time a waltz.

As he took her into his arms, she gazed up at him, something in her eyes affecting him in a way he did not wish to delve into any deeper. "You look particularly lovely this evening, my dear. That color brings out the blue in your eyes."

She sucked in a breath, and once again her cheeks were tinged with a lovely shade of rose. He was reluctant to leave her, lest the biddies begin to gossip and hurl remarks in her direction. He could stay by her side, but that seemed a bit drastic and much removed from their normal practice. After the music ended, he kissed her hand, escorted her to her usual group of friends, and retired to the card room. Since it was generally accepted that a married man not stick by his wife's side, lest he be considered "besotted," she would stay in the ballroom with the other matrons. She would often leave before him, so he would not see her until dinner the following evening.

***

The next afternoon Eugenia browsed the shelves of Webster's bookstore on Bond Street. This was her favorite time of the week, when she allowed herself the luxury of wasting time looking at books and picking out two or three that she would purchase for her growing library. She didn't add them to the main library, since Devon would not want to be disturbed by her entering to find a book while he was working.

The previous night's ball had not been as difficult as she'd thought it might be. Since Mrs. Forestor had been a known courtesan, her name would not be mentioned in polite society with innocent young ladies present. She'd caught some knowing looks from the older women present and stumbled upon two ladies in the retiring room having a robust chat that quickly came to an end when Eugenia entered the room.

Her attention returned to the book shelves as her gloved fingers moved over the books, looking for something different. She pulled a book from the shelf, and the binding snagged another one alongside it that tumbled to the floor. Her eye caught the title in bold black letters.

Secrets of the Bedchamber.

She bent to retrieve it, and the tome fell open in her hands. Her eyes grew wide and she gasped before snapping it shut, glancing furtively around to confirm no one was nearby.

Assured of the emptiness of the store and with the book clutched in her hand, she hurried to the back of the shelves to make certain no one saw her, and slowly opened the book. Heat rose to her cheeks. A drawing of a naked couple in a very awkward position almost made her giggle. Did people really move their limbs into that sort of an arrangement?

As she flipped through the pages, she noted it contained advice on how to conduct oneself with regard to sexual concourse between men and women. She licked her suddenly dry lips, her heart thumping as she read the words and considered the additional drawings. The one with the woman on her knees in front of a naked man, with her...*Oh, my!*

Her hands shook and her breathing increased. Heat shot from her middle as she attempted to hold in a giggle. The Ice Queen was melting...

I must have this book.

The thought flashed through her mind without consideration. Of course the problem she faced was getting it out of the store. It hardly bore thinking of her embarrassment if Mr. Webster noticed the title and knew the contents. She chewed on her lip—very unqueenly—and pondered how to take possession of the knowledge in the book.

Mayhap she could come in every day and huddle in the corner of the store and take notes? No. She had to *own* this book.

The idea popped into her head so quickly she questioned all the years she had done everything the right way. Never once had she succumbed to improper behavior. Until now.

She would steal it.

Not really steal it, of course. She would slip it into her reticule and purchase two other books. Then, she would distract Mr. Webster with conversation and leave money on the counter for the naughty book. Yes. She would do it!

Her heart pounding fiercely, she took note of her surroundings and almost swooned at her impertinence. Not only was she buying a scandalous book, she was actually tucking it into her reticule so she could walk out of the store with Mr. Webster completely unaware of her actions.

She cringed to think what her mother would say. Shoving that to the back of her mind and taking a deep breath to calm her nerves, she selected two books and headed to the front of the store, the weight of the stolen book banging against her leg as she walked. Good heavens, she'd never done anything at all like this in her whole life. How did thieves function every day? She was a bundle of nerves.

"Good afternoon, Lady Devon. Did you find books for your pleasure?" The older man greeted her as she laid her books on the counter.

For your pleasure?

She forced down a giggle. Did he know she had tucked the scandalous book into her reticule? Why had he used that particular phrase? With a lavender-scented handkerchief, she gently dabbed her upper lip where beads of moisture had formed. Lord, she never perspired. A life of crime was certainly not for her.

"Yes. Thank you, Mr. Webster." Rattled even further by her shaky voice, she shoved the two books across the counter. "I will take these, if you please."

He reached for the books and grinned. "I had no idea you were interested in the Aborigines, my lady."

She gasped at the title of the book the man held out to her.

The Habits and Culture of the Aborigines by Lord Stephen Manors.

Dear heavens, was that the book she'd picked up?
"Yes, as a matter of fact, I thought …well…to…to broaden my knowledge of the world," she finished lamely.

"Very commendable, my lady." He wrote some figures on a piece of paper and added them up. "That will be fifteen shillings."

Eugenia stared at him aghast. How could she go into her reticule for her money? She wanted to stomp her foot at forgetting this part of the transaction. How would she do that with the man standing there staring at her?

Heat rose to her face until she felt as though she would combust. "Um, this is so silly." She gave him a strained laugh. "But it seems I left my money at home. Could you please place this on my account—if I have one, that is?" She'd always paid for her books. In some small way it made her feel as though she had some control over her life, even though her pin money came from her husband.

"Of course, of course, my lady. Lord Devon maintains an account, and I will be happy to add your purchase to his."

"Th-th-thank you." One more swipe on her upper lip with her handkerchief. Since she could not go into her reticule for her money, she was indeed flat-out stealing the naughty book, after all. Before she could give too much consideration to her actions, she fled the store.

Head down, she hurried away, her mind in a jumble, not really sure which way she was walking. She had even left her poor maid, Sally, still browsing the shelves of the bookstore. She'd walked only—nay, practically ran—about a half a block when she nearly crashed into a pair of fawn breeches, silver waistcoat, and dark brown jacket. Her eyes climbed up the figure to meet a pair of very familiar dark brown eyes. His brows rose, and he gaped at her. "Eugenia? Is everything all right, my dear?"

***

Devon stared down at his wife. *His flustered wife.*

Something he'd never seen in six months of courting and five months of marriage. She was panting heavily, there was a light film of perspiration on her upper lip, and her face was as red as the apples being sold from the fruit cart across the street.

She regarded him, her mouth agape. Something else he'd never seen before. The poor woman was obviously in a bit of distress. "Eugenia? Is something amiss?"

Eugenia shook her head, almost as if to clear it. "No. No, nothing at all, my lord. I am fine. Just taking a stroll." She cast him a grin that would give a small child nightmares.

"I don't wish to contradict you, my dear, but you are flushed and seem out of sorts, and galloping along, rather than strolling. Perhaps I might escort you to Gunter's for an ice?"

She glanced at the reticule that dangled from her wrist, and her red face paled. What the devil was going on with his usually unflappable wife? "Yes, my lord. That would be quite pleasant."

Devon extended his elbow, which she gripped, glancing over her shoulder as if expecting to be snatched away. Very strange.

Due to the temperature of the day there was a considerable crowd outside the store. He escorted Eugenia to a small table under a tree where the air was cooler. That might help to calm her. He shook his head. Never had he experienced a need to calm Eugenia. She was...well, he had never liked the moniker the *ton* had bestowed on her. The Ice Queen.

She appeared a bit more composed when he joined her with the ice. She fanned herself and smiled brightly at him as he placed the ice in front of her. "Are you feeling better?"

"Yes. Much." Why did he think she was lying? She kept glancing at her reticule as if she expected it to jump up and bite her. When she took a taste of her ice, a small piece stayed on the corner of her mouth. Distracted, she didn't seem to even notice. He motioned with his finger to his mouth.

"What?"

"Your mouth."

"What about my mouth?"

"You have a piece of ice stuck there."

Instead of reaching for the handkerchief she always kept in her reticule, she simply moved her tongue out and scooped up the piece of ice.

All his blood rushed to his groin.

What the devil is the matter with me? This was his proper wife he was feeling lust for, not some doxy. As they continued with their treat, he seemed to see her for the first time since their encounter. Her hair wasn't quite as perfect as it usually was. There remained two bright spots on her cheeks, and the sight of her running her tongue around her lips to catch the ice had him realizing how very plump and inviting those lips were.

Of course he'd kissed those lips before. Certainly not in the way he wished to devour them now. But their copulating had always been what was proper between a husband and wife. Not wanting to upset her delicate nature, he'd always visited her in the dark, offered a few perfunctory kisses before he entered her, then quickly took his leave so as not to disturb her rest. Exactly the way he'd been instructed by his father before he'd ever thought of taking a wife,

"Remember, son, a wife is a special person with tender sensibilities. You must not upset her by treating her like a light-skirt. Protect your wife, show her the proper respect, and slake your lust on a mistress."

Perhaps he was merely fascinated by her lips because of the five months he'd been without his normal sexual release. Not that he had no control over his lusty inclinations. He was not a young pup, but a man fully grown, capable of behaving as a gentleman with his wife, whom he had always treated with the utmost kindness and consideration.

"If you are finished with your ice, my dear, I shall escort you home. Is your maid with you?"

She licked her lips once again and looked at him with surprise. "Oh, dear. Yes, I believe she is. Though I might have left her back at the carriage, waiting for me."

Odd. To his knowledge, his wife had never before misplaced a servant. "I will have the footman with me instruct her to return to the house, and I will see you home in the carriage I brought."

"That is not necessary, my lord." She fumbled with her reticule as she attempted to rise. "I am sure you have other business for which you need attend."

"Not at all. I shall be happy to see you home."

Still ruminating on the curious behavior of Eugenia, he extended his arm and they walked away from Gunter's to their carriage. After only a few steps, it came to his notice the sound of something heavy slapping against her leg as they walked along. It sounded to his ears as if she carried a heavy object in her reticule. When he glanced down at the small bag she patted her upper lip with a lavender-scented handkerchief and turned quite red in the face.

"Is there something in your reticule that I can carry for you?"

"No!" She snatched the bag from her wrist and held it protectively over her bosom. "I purchased some candies and might feel the need to have one." She darted a glance at him. "Soon."

They reached his carriage, and he helped her in. He eyed her as they rolled away from Bond Street. She continued to clutch the reticule to her person, her face going from bright red to pale white. If he didn't know his wife so well, he would think she had something in her reticule she did not wish him to see.

Doubtful. Eugenia was nothing, if not predictable.

Want to read the rest of the story? You can purchase *Seducing the Marquess* at most online retailers. Visit my website for more information or follow this link: http://bit.ly/2giSDk7

ABOUT THE AUTHOR

Callie Hutton, the *USA Today* bestselling author of *The Elusive Wife*, writes both Western Historical and Regency romance, with "historic elements and sensory details" (*The Romance Reviews*). She also pens an occasional contemporary or two. Callie lives in Oklahoma with several rescue dogs and her top cheerleader husband of many years. Her family also includes her daughter, son, daughter-in-law and twin grandsons affectionately known as "The Twinadoes."

Callie loves to hear from readers. Contact her directly at calliehutton11@gmail.com or find her online at www.calliehutton.com. Sign up for her newsletter to receive information on new releases, appearances, contests and exclusive subscriber content. Visit her on Facebook, Twitter and Goodreads.

Callie Hutton has written more than 25 books. For a complete listing, go to www.calliehutton.com/books

Praise for books by Callie Hutton

A Wife by Christmas

"A *Wife by Christmas* is the reason why we read romance...the perfect story for any season." --The Romance Reviews Top Pick

The Elusive Wife

"I loved this book and you will too. Jason is a hottie & Oliva is the kind of woman we'd all want as a friend. Read it!" --Cocktails and Books

"In my experience I've had a few hits but more misses with historical romance so I was really pleasantly surprised to be hooked from the start by obviously good writing." --Book Chick City

"The historic elements and sensory details of each scene make the story come to life, and certainly helps immerse the reader in the world that Olivia and Jason share." --The Romance Reviews

"You will not want to miss *The Elusive Wife*." --My Book Addiction

"…it was a well written plot and the characters were likeable." --Night Owl Reviews

A Run for Love

"An exciting, heart-warming Western love story!" --*NY Times* bestselling author Georgina Gentry

"I loved this book!!! I read the BEST historical romance last night…It's called *A Run For Love*.: --*NY Times* bestselling author Sharon Sala

"This is my first Callie Hutton story, but it certainly won't be my last." --The Romance Reviews

A Prescription for Love

"There was love, romance, angst, some darkness, laughter, hope and despair." --RomCon

"I laughed out loud at some of the dialogue and situations. I think you will enjoy this story by Callie Hutton." --Night Owl Reviews

An Angel in the Mail

"…a warm fuzzy sensuous read. I didn't put it down until I was done." --Sizzling Hot Reviews

Visit www.calliehutton.com for more information.

Made in United States
Orlando, FL
26 March 2022